# Abbey's Tale

## by

## Katherine McDermott

**Abbey's Tale**

Cover Art by *Kim Mendoza*

The Wild Rose Press, Inc.
PO Box 708
Adams Basin, NY 14410-0708
Visit us at www.thewildrosepress.com

Publishing History
First American Rose Edition, 2016
Print ISBN 978-1-5092-1185-2
Digital ISBN 978-1-5092-1186-9

Published in the United States of America

**Abigail gasped and sucked cold salt water**
into her nose and sinuses. It stung and made her eyes tear as she choked it back up. She flailed at the water, trying to remember what her father had taught her about swimming as a child, but the lessons had taken place in a calm inlet not a tempest.

"Papa!" she screamed. "Papa!"

Could he hear her above the roar of the sea and the pouring rain? She felt something churning the surface of the water.

*My God, a shark?!*

Thunder cracked overhead. Teeth closed around her upper right arm. She screamed and reached out with her left hand, but the head she touched had hair, short hair, and she felt a long, floppy ear—a dog.

The heavy wool cape dragged her down. She tried to clutch the dog, but it let go its grip. *I'm pulling it under too.* She untied the cape at her throat and let it disappear into the surf. Her teeth chattered in her head, and she felt cold, as cold as death. *So this is how it feels to die.*

## Kudos for Katherine McDermott

Katherine McDermott is the award-winning author of *HIDING* (also published by The Wild Rose Press, Inc.). She received the Daphne du Maurier Award for Suspense from RWA, a SOLA Award, and an award for excellence in writing from The Blue Ridge Writers Conference. She teaches English at Trident Technical College.

## Dedication

To my mother
who took me to libraries as a child
and encouraged a love for reading.

"Kindness is the language which the deaf can hear and the blind can see." ~Mark Twain

Chapter One

*Maine, 1869*

Abigail ran her sensitive fingers over the driftwood figures from the sill of the bay window with sensuous delight. She caressed the leaping dolphin with its smooth side, angled dorsal fin, and sloping tail. Her forefinger traced the harlequin-like smile beneath its bottlenose, and a smile widened her own lips. She stroked the frolicking sea otter which lay on its back holding a starfish playfully with its front paws. The driftwood gull soared in flight with outstretched wings.

*What must the man be like who can carve such beautiful things?* Through his work, she'd seen the world as never before. *Who is he, and why does he so rarely leave the island? Why the self-imposed exile?*

She listened to the low hiss of the leaping flames and cheerful crackle of burning logs from her seat in the gooseneck rocker near the fire.

The yeasty aroma of baking bread drew Abigail back to present. Dropping her wooden treasures into the roomy pockets of her apron, she moved to the cast-iron stove where she adeptly withdrew the bread pan with a frayed pot holder. She transported it to the table to cool. Then opening the glass front of the pendulum clock, she felt the position of the brass hands. The smaller hand rested on the raised Roman numeral V. The larger pointed to X. Her father would soon be back from his mail delivery and his monthly trip to Lighthouse Island.

Acutely sensitive to sounds, she heard the clam chowder bubbling on the stove and stirred it. Its salty, fishy aroma was like the sea itself. The plush-sided cat brushed gently but insistently against her skirts.

"You're hungry, aren't you, Charlie?" Abigail took scraps of cod from the pot in the sink and fed the indolent tom.

The cheerful jangling of keys rattled in the lock as the front door of the gray Cape Cod cottage creaked open. Cold air burst into the room.

"Abbey, girl, I'm home," Marion Morrison sang out.

She crossed to embrace him. His scratchy beard, chilly and damp, prickled against her smooth cheeks. The breath of frosty salt air lingered in the foyer.

"Have you brought another carving?" Abbey asked eagerly.

"You're still like a little girl," he chided. "Of course, I've brought something. Don't I always?" She reached out and received a carving. Her fingers ran over it gingerly.

"What is it?" she asked slightly mystified.

"It's his dog, a massive, chocolate-colored Labrador retriever he calls Bailey."

"Yes, I thought it might be a dog or perhaps a wolf. How does he decide what to carve?"

"He says he sees the image within the bend of the wood."

"That's an unusual gift. I'm surprised he's willing to part with a carving of his pet."

"Oh, he has several statues of the dog." Marion

took off his coat and hung it on a peg, then placed his hat and muffler beside it.

"Doesn't he get lonely out there on the island with no one else around?"

"I think he prefers it that way, and he stays busy." Marion moved before the fire place. "He always gets me to bring out books and newspapers."

"What is he reading now?" Abigail asked, for she had read many Braille novels. She was daily thankful to the fifteen-year-old French boy, Louis Braille, who had invented the system while at the National Institute for Blind Youth in Paris.

"I took him the Charles Dickens novel *A Tale of Two Cities.*"

"The French Revolution, such a tumultuous time." She had not told her father that she'd cried copious tears at the end when Sidney Carton had sacrificed his life for the happiness of the woman he secretly loved. Would she ever experience such love?

"Is supper ready?"

"I'll take up the chowder. The bread's cooling on the table. Would you please slice it?"

She filled two pewter mugs with cider, placed them on the roughhewn table, and returned to the stove where she ladled up the flavorful broth and then positioned two steaming bowls between the place settings. Her father reached across to take her right hand once she was seated, and she bowed her head.

"For these and all thy many blessings, we are truly grateful. Amen," Marion intoned.

Cold rain pattered against the window as they ate, but inside, the house felt snug and warm. After they'd eaten, Marion took his pipe down from the mantel, tamped in the aromatic tobacco, and lit it. In the kitchen, Abigail washed up the dishes as she took in the fragrant smoke. Then carefully, she returned each carving to its place on the wide sill of the bay window in the dining room.

****

On Lighthouse Island off the rugged Maine coast, the rain had not yet started, but it fell like gray ribbons on the mainland. Jeremy McKetcheon squatted on the stoop of his red clapboard house and, with a dull knife, scaled the two cod he'd caught that afternoon. The black Lab watched him with keen interest, its pink tongue protruding between its canine teeth as it panted. Jeremy reached over and scratched Bailey's head and neck.

*Dogs are great animals. They never judge by appearances the way humans do.* The dog licked his chin and wagged its club of a tail.

"The sea's violent tonight. I'll light the lamp sooner than usual." He often spoke aloud to the dog.

Stepping inside, Jeremy quickly pan-fried the fish and took his plate up the thirty-eight steps to the lantern room and parapet. He lit the first order Fresnel lamp. With its increased reflective powers over the old Argand light, it could be seen up to twenty miles at sea helping sailors navigate the treacherous Maine coast.

In the dimming dusk, Jeremy viewed the small town of Arbor on the mainland—nothing more than a cluster of houses and fishing wharves. Most of the inhabitants were more at home on their boats where they earned their livings taking lobsters from traps and fish from the sea. The town did not even have a church or a school, though worship took place on the common when weather permitted and in Marion Morrison's house when snow and rain fell. In addition to being the mail carrier and a lobsterman, Marion also served as the lay pastor of a mixed group of Protestant denominations. Most parents taught their own children to read and do sums at home.

Ever faithful, Bailey padded up the stairs behind his master. After his cursory and customary circle around the parapet, the dog lay down resting his enormous head on his front paws and slumbered.

Jeremy took up one of the twisted pieces of driftwood he'd collected on the beach and turned it around in his hands, then pulled his carving knife from its sheath. Like the whalers from earlier in the century who filled their idle hours with scrimshaw engravings on whalebone, Jeremy plied his art. Wood shavings curled at his feet as the image took shape. Usually a realistic carver, this time his mind took a fanciful turn as he created a winding sea serpent.

Outside, the wind howled, and waves crashed upon the rocks. His thick wool jacket and scarf kept him warm, but as the hours passed, he grew drowsy. His chin slumped. Whistling bullets shrieked by, and booming cannon fire thundered. The earth trembled as men screamed out, clutched their chests, or raised their arms to the sky imploring God to end their misery. Crimson stains spread across uniforms. An incoming cannonball beheaded a Union captain astride his war horse.

Jeremy dropped and scampered along the ground like a lizard. Severed limbs, arms, legs, and booted feet littered the earth as Jeremy crawled toward his friend Branson. But his friend's eyes were frozen in a shocked stare. A perfectly round bullet hole pierced his forehead.

Jeremy wanted to vomit; he gagged and woke himself. Shaking his head as though dispelling ghosts, he stood on wobbly legs and walked out onto the parapet into the bracing sea air. The clouds had moved off, and white stars dotted the moonlit night. How he hated and dreaded sleep. It had become a plague to be avoided at all costs.

*Perhaps another cup of coffee.*

\*\*\*\*

"When are you going to take me to the island?" Abigail asked at breakfast. "Did you tell the carver that I want to meet him?"

"No. I told you, he's a very private man."

"But why is he such a hermit, Papa? He never even comes to town. You take him the supplies that the Light Keeping Service sends. You're the only person he ever sees. How can anyone stand to be so lonely?"

"He has his reasons." Marion took the tin plate of scrambled eggs that Abigail brought him.

"But what are they?"

Marion sighed. "What an inquisitive daughter you've become. You're almost as bad as my sister, your aunt Agnes." But he quickly saw from her crestfallen expression that he'd hurt her feelings. *A daughter needs a mother.*

He sighed audibly.

"He was in the war," he said in a conciliatory fashion. "Not that he wanted to be. He emigrated from Ireland and was sending money back home to his family. When the son of some wealthy Boston merchant got drafted, the family paid him to go in the

6

son's place. He needed the money."

"It wasn't really his war to fight," she said indignant. "He only wanted to keep his family alive."

"Wanted to save up passage to bring his sister over, but she died before he could get the money together."

"Is he a Catholic then?"

"I imagine so. He's a man of few words. It's taken me two years to get this much out of him. He doesn't like people poking around in his past."

"I'm not poking around," Abigail defended herself. "And I'm not a gossip like Aunt Aggie, judging everyone and spreading tales around."

"I know you're not. I shouldn't have made the comparison."

Slightly mollified, Abigail brought her father a cup of coffee with cream and sugar.

"I just want to tell him in person how much I enjoy his carvings and take him some cranberry scones."

"I'll speak to him next month when I go out. I wouldn't dream of surprising him without his permission. But don't set your hopes too high. It's very likely he'll decline your visit."

\*\*\*\*

Jeremy and Bailey dug in the soft mud at low tide, Jeremy with a long-handled shovel and Bailey with his webbed front paws. Whenever they unearthed a good-sized clam, Jeremy tossed it into a wooden bucket. Bailey got distracted by a crab moving sideways across the beach, its claws up and ready for action. The dog gamboled around it barking and sniffing until the crab pinched his nose. Bailey yelped and backed up.

"Come here, Bailey," Jeremy commanded.

He lifted the full bucket, and they headed to the

house where Jeremy cleaned the mollusks and steamed them open.

"Nothing like good salty Down East clams," he told the dog after popping one into his mouth.

Bailey looked at him with shining brown eyes of adoration.

"Try one." Jeremy held a clam in his palm. The dog snatched it up and wagged his tail.

When he'd washed up all the dishes, Jeremy took *A Tale of Two Cities* down from its perch on the mantelpiece, lit a lantern, and sat down to read. He was up to the part where Dr. Manette had been rescued from the Bastille and reunited with his daughter. He allowed himself to read until five o'clock before going up to light the lamp in the tower.

Chapter Two

Nearly a month had passed since Abigail had received the carving of the Labrador. Her father paid the carver a small amount for each piece. *The light keeper probably thinks they are toys for a child. Maybe the keeper doesn't even know my father has a daughter.*

She sat in the gooseneck rocker knitting a hat from green yarn. At least, she'd been told the yarn was green by Mrs. Stapleton in the mercantile. Funny thing color—she had no idea what it was. The only store in Arbor, the mercantile, sold cloth, buttons, shoes, sewing notions, hair pins, combs, and brushes. For men there were razors, boots, nets, fishing gear, suspenders, belts, pipes, and tobacco. The dry goods included coffee, flour, tea, sugar, cornmeal, and spices.

Sometimes Mrs. Stapleton bought extra eggs from Abigail who had gathered them from the speckled black and white hens her father kept in the coop behind the house. She always avoided the strutting rooster, an ornery creature with sharp spurs. Sometimes, she got eggs from Aunt Agatha and Uncle Jack's farm up the hill. Abigail tried to give her father a hearty breakfast before sending him off to check his lobster traps.

Tired of knitting, she carefully finished a row and set her needles and yarn aside.

The clock struck nine. The store would be open. She crossed to the bookshelf and located the third book to the right on the second shelf. Her father always kept several dollars there for household expenses. She removed the book, flipped to page ten, and removed two crisp bills. They were always in one dollar denominations, so that she would know the amount.

The store sat directly across the street, an immediate left when she hit the boardwalk and forty-three steps forward to the door. A little bell above the entrance tinkled when she pushed it open.

"Abigail, it's good to see you." Mrs. Stapleton greeted her from behind the counter. "How can I help you this morning?"

"I'm looking for cranberries, flour, and sugar. Oh, and do you have any buttermilk? I'm planning to make scones."

"We have some nice dried berries that will moisten up if you soak them in water.

And Mr. Odom brought in some buttermilk yesterday. It's cooling in the cellar out back. Let me fetch it, and then I'll measure and weigh the rest of the ingredients."

"Thank you." Abigail walked to the back and fingered the bolts of cloth there. She liked to feel the different textures. She heard the bell tinkle as another customer entered.

"Why, is that my niece?" Abigail recognized the voice of her own aunt Aggie. Staccato heels clicked across the wooden floor as she approached. Suddenly, she was enveloped in a smothering hug.

"How are you, dear? I haven't seen you lately. You look thin."

*You always say that,* Abbey thought as her aunt's plump breasts pressed against her. "How's Uncle

Jack?"

"Grumpy as ever. He's arthritic, and his fingers are sore from mending his fishing nets. How is my brother?"

"Still working all the time."

"Miss Morrison," Myrtle Stapleton said, re-entering the store. "Your order is ready."

"Shall I walk you over?" Agatha asked Abigail.

"No, I can navigate the store on my own." She tried to hide her annoyance. As she reached the counter, Abigail asked Mrs. Stapleton what she owed.

"Seventy-five cents."

Abigail handed her one of the bills and then fingered the quarter returned to her.

\*\*\*\*

"Try one," Abbey told her father. She handed him a plate with a cranberry scone and a cup of hot chamomile tea with a bit of cream.

Marion bit into the moist pastry with its chewy fruit.

"Quite good," he announced.

"I'm going to put eight scones in a tin for the carver. You are still taking me tomorrow?"

"Yes, yes," Marion said. His resistance had been worn away like sand on a beach eroded by the constant motion of the tides.

"Take him some of your spiced tea," he said. "Hopefully he'll forgive our invasion of his privacy."

Abigail picked up Charlie who was rubbing against her legs and scratched his head. His whiskers tickled her arm. She could barely contain her enthusiasm.

That night she got little sleep as she anticipated the visit. What other creatures had the carver fashioned that would let her see the world?

At dawn, she arose before her father, dressed warmly, and carefully put her long auburn hair up with pins and combs. After a breakfast of oatmeal with brown sugar, Marion insisted on enjoying his pipe before sorting the mail. He delivered the local mail first while Abigail paced about the house impatiently.

"What took so long?" she asked when he returned.

"Your aunt and uncle had to tell me all their latest ailments. Can you fix me a sandwich before we leave?"

Abbey sighed but acquiesced and made herself one as well. Finally, they walked to the wharf, Abigail with her arm hooked through her father's.

"How's the weather?' she asked.

"Some gray clouds along the horizon, but we should get there before the storm."

He helped her into the rocking dinghy and situated her in the bow section. Then he untethered the ropes that held them to the wharf, sat on the middle plank, and put the oars in the oarlocks. He pulled against the choppy surf as Abigail listened to the lonely cries of gulls overhead. She had carefully secured the tin of scones and jar of tea beneath the seat.

Marion stopped to chat with other fishermen from time to time further delaying their arrival at Lighthouse Island. He began to row in earnest intensity as he saw the approaching storm. Even Abbey heard the distant rumble and felt the lurching of the boat over the waves. She clung to sides with white-knuckled intensity.

\*\*\*\*

Ominous thunderclouds gathered overhead. Torrential rain began to pour, so Jeremy went inside from the parapet to the lamp room, grabbed his telescope, and trained it on the heaving sea. A blue dinghy—perhaps the postman's—bucked the waves like a bronco, and someone rode with him, someone wearing a dark, hooded wool cloak. It must be the daughter Marion had mentioned.

"Come on, Bailey!"

The dog barked and bounded down the circuitous staircase ahead of him. Jeremy raced to the shore where his own rowboat lay tied to a post and beached on the sand beyond the high tide mark. He untied it and slid it across the damp shore. Baily jumped in as Jeremy steadied the vessel and walked it past the rocks and up to his boot tops in the cold water. Then being careful to put both arms across to the opposite side of the boat, he dragged himself over the side and scrambled aboard.

Sitting in the middle astride a wooden plank, he pulled at the two oars using all his strength to head in the direction of the floundering mail boat. At the bow, Bailey continued to bark loudly and then looked back at him with a worried whimper.

Jeremy watched in horror as a huge, foaming wave lifted the mailman and his passenger from their swamped vessel and heaved them into the churning surf. Marion bashed his head against the rocks, and blood spread down one side of his face from a gash above his right eyebrow. Unconscious, the mailman slipped beneath the surface.

"Bailey! Go get him!"

The Labrador searched Jeremy's eyes for a moment.

"Go on! Get him!" Jeremy commanded.

The dog leapt from the rescue boat, plunged into the ocean, and headed toward the rocks where Marion's body had sunk.

Jeremy rowed toward the hooded figure. She fought her tangled skirts and floundered against the waves trying to stay afloat. Jeremy kicked off his boots and then went over the side. He held onto the boat with one hand and gave powerful scissor kicks with his muscular legs to reach her. Praying that his thigh and calf muscles did not cramp in the ice cold water, he moved forward with strong, steady arm strokes.

\*\*\*\*

Abigail gasped and sucked cold salt water into her nose and sinuses. It stung and made her eyes tear as she choked it back up. She flailed at the water, trying to remember what her father had taught her about swimming as a child, but the lessons had taken place in a calm inlet not a tempest.

"Papa!" she screamed. "Papa!"

Could he hear her above the roar of the sea and the pouring rain? She felt something churning the surface of the water.

*My God, a shark?!*

Thunder cracked overhead. Teeth closed around her upper right arm. She screamed and reached out with her left hand, but the head she touched had hair, short hair, and she felt a long, floppy ear—a dog.

The heavy wool cape dragged her down. She tried to clutch the dog, but it let go its grip. *I'm pulling it under too.* She untied the cape at her throat and let it disappear into the surf. Her teeth chattered in her head, and she felt cold, as cold as death. *So this is how it feels to die.*

No longer able to struggle, she slipped beneath the surface.

**\*\*\*\***

Jeremy dove down into the depths; his fingers grasped lank seaweed. No, he realized, it was her hair, silky and wet. He gripped a handful and brought her up to the surface, then managed to heave her limp body into the lifeboat. He dove again near the rocks where Marion had gone down and disappeared in the foaming surf. Five times he went under, but he did not find him. Dizzy and disoriented, he knew that one could die from hypothermia in such cold water. He resurfaced and gulped in the cold air. Pain seared his lungs.

Bailey dog-paddled to him and grasped his upper arm in his mouth. The persistent dog urgently pulled him back to the dinghy. Jeremy summoned his last bit of strength and heaved himself aboard and then helped the soaked dog inside. He checked the girl in the bottom of the boat and compressed her chest several times with locked hands. He turned her head sideways; water gurgled from her throat. She took in a breath. Then tugging against the oars with all his might, he headed back to shore.

There he lifted the woman from the battered dinghy and stumbled to the lighthouse. The stove had kept the building warm, but Jeremy could not get his teeth to stop chattering. Bailey shook himself all over sending a small shower of salt water to form a puddle on the pine board floor.

Completely unconscious, the girl lay limp on the rag rug before the stove. She drew in a breath, then let out a low moan. Her eyes did not open as he removed her outer garments leaving only a thin slip clinging to her slender body and rounded breasts. He retrieved a heavy wool blanket from the bedroom and wrapped her up tightly.

Only then did he take care of himself. Returning to the bedroom and stripping to his skin, he toweled off and pulled on dry breeches and a thick cable knit sweater. His own body continued to shake. He went back to the iron potbellied stove and lay down on the hard floor next to it panting and trying to catch his breath. Gradually, his trembling subsided. His teeth quit chattering; he stood on shaky legs. Retrieving the kettle with trembling hands, he filled it with water and put it atop the stove to boil.

When it simmered and steam arose, he fixed himself a cup of strong coffee and having drunk it, refilled the cup, and knelt next to the girl on the floor. Her eyes fluttered slightly, as he got her to take a few sips.

"I—I just want to sleep," she murmured. He let her lie back down and then went to fetch a pillow from the bed to place under her head.

He gave Bailey a bowl of water, but Jeremy knew that he had to make sure the light in the tower stayed afire.

"You stay and watch her," he commanded Bailey. In the bedroom, yet again, he put on heavy wool socks, a jacket, and long scarf before making his long trek up the stairs.

The night seemed endless. Rain and sleet pelted the windows of the lantern room. And from time to time, he could not help dropping off into restless slumber. He was in deep sleep when dawn peeked above the horizon turning the storm clouds orange and magenta, and he was startled awake by Bailey's wet tongue licking his cheeks. The dog bounded down the stairs before Jeremy could gather his wits.

For a moment, he couldn't remember what had happened, and then the horror of the previous night crept over him. He realized he had to tell the woman, who he assumed was Marion's daughter, that her father had drowned. *My God, Marion is gone.*

Mechanically, he extinguished the flames and cleaned soot from the windows.

****

Downstairs, Abigail awoke stiff and sore. She blinked her heavy, swollen lids. She realized that beneath the blanket, she had little on. *Who took my dress?* Her lips tasted salty and felt shriveled and chapped.

"Papa?" she called out. "Papa?"

She remembered calling for him in the cold surf. Surely, he had rescued her, pulled her from the water. She sat up, but when she did her head hurt, and she felt nauseated.

"Papa?" She strained her ears. She could hear the low hiss of a fire and the crackle of burning wood. She sensed the direction from which the heat emanated and smelled the smoke of a wood stove.

Then she heard a slight whimpering.

"Papa, I'm all right." She stretched out her shaking arms toward the sound.

A cold, damp nose startled her. She heard sniffing and recognized the panting of a dog. Rising on wobbly legs, she tried to get her bearings.

Footsteps descending stairs echoed to her left.

Confused, she moved slowly in a circle reaching out her arms to detect obstructions. She remembered a dog, coming to her in the water. She'd been thrown from the boat. And her father? What had happened to him?

She pulled the blanket closer around her. Suddenly, like a blow to the gut, she knew her father was gone. Yet somehow he still existed, still protected her from afar.

She knelt and touched the dog. His warm body comforted her.

\*\*\*\*

Jeremy stopped at the bottom step and watched the girl in the pale gray light of dawn. How forlorn she looked, her waist-length hair hanging in limp strands down her back and over her shoulders. But she'd been on her feet, a good sign. *What do I say? How do I tell her? Should I postpone it?* He decided to get some food into her. He'd avoid telling her as long as possible.

"Morning," he said. "I'm Jeremy McKetcheon. I'm the light keeper here."

She nodded absentmindedly, turning back to the warmth of the stove fire behind the grated iron door.

*She's still in shock. Or she's frightened by my face.*

He ducked into the bedroom and retrieved her dress which had dried by the fireplace.

"Your clothes are dry if ya want ta change in the bedroom." She looked in his direction.

"It's through that door." He indicated, handing her the dress.

She stood uncertainly and took the clothes with one hand. The other held the blanket tightly around her body. Her movements were so unsure, at first he thought her completely addled. And then reality hit him as she groped forward stretching out her hands.

"You're blind?"

"Yes." She nodded.

"I didn't know. Marion, I mean, your father never told me."

"No, he wouldn't have," she replied. "He never burdened others with his troubles."

Jeremy took her arm and led her to the bedroom, there letting her feel the four-post bed with the star-pattern quilt. He walked her around the room.

"The pitcher and basin are here near the window." He let her touch the porcelain. "The chamber pot is under the bed. The wardrobe is here."

She reached for the knob and found it.

"There isn't much else, so I'll leave ya ta ya privacy."

"Thank you." She clutched her dress like an abandoned waif.

Where the blanket opened in the front, he saw her thin, wrinkled slip.

He left the room, and while she changed, he heated a pot of oatmeal and tossed a beef bone into Bailey's dish. When she reappeared in the doorway fully dressed, he jumped up to lead her to the rough-hewn table where he pulled out a chair. She felt for the seat and sat down.

"Ya really ought ta eat something. I've warmed up some porridge."

He put two steaming bowls of thick porridge on the table. She easily found the spoon but paused.

"Shall we ask grace?" she questioned.

It had been years since Jeremy had prayed. Of course, there had been desperate prayers during his war years, but when he had awakened and seen his mutilated face for the first time, something had died inside him. He had not prayed since. Now the most innocent and beautiful girl he had ever seen was asking him to pray just hours after almost losing her own life.

"Would—would ya?" He stumbled over the words.

She bowed her head and closed her eyes, even though she had lived in darkness all her life. In a melodious voice, she said the Lord's Prayer in a simplistic, child-like manner.

"Our Father, who art in heaven…"

He found himself joining in the words. He was glad that she could not see his amazed stare or his hideous deformity. She picked up her spoon, dipped it into the oatmeal, and blew on it to cool it. Then she tasted it.

"It's very good," she murmured in a distracted manner.

"I don't even know ya name."

"Abigail."

"Abigail," he repeated.

"My mother chose the name because it means gift from God. My parents thought for many years that they couldn't have children, and then I was born. I was born blind, but it never mattered to them."

"Ya father told me he had a daughter, but I guess, I mean, I thought ya were a child."

"He told me about you," she answered. "And I have seen the world through your beautiful carvings, dolphins and otters and birds in flight. All so amazing. I've seen the world through my fingers."

Jeremy stared at the delicate hand that held the spoon poised above the bowl of porridge.

"Ya father was…was my best friend," he stammered, but he did not tell her Marion was his only friend. Suddenly, he wondered if her father had ever told her about the lighthouse keeper's hideous face. He hoped that the postman had kept that secret as well as he had kept his daughter's.

"I notice that you say 'was.' He didn't survive last night, did he?" Her chin trembled slightly. She set down her spoon. Tears trembled on her lower lashes.

*What should he say? How should he phrase it?*

"No, he didna. I tried. Believe me! I dove for him over and over again. But I failed him."

A long moment of silence lingered as neither tried to fill the void.

"I can feel his spirit here as if he's watching over me still," Abbey said, choking a little on the words.

Jeremy found himself looking about the room as though he expected to see Marion. But there was no one, and the only sound was the lonely whistle of the wind.

*Maybe the blind see things the sighted can't.*

"I let him down," Jeremy said, his own voice ragged.

"I know you tried." Abbey reached over and gently felt for his hand. She gave it a squeeze.

Slowly, the storm subsided. But outside the window, the ocean churned and foamed as waves slapped against the rocks.

"It's too dangerous to take ya home," he said. "But the people on shore must be worried about ya. Ya husband, ya friends."

"I have no husband," Abigail said. "I live, I mean lived, with my father. No one will miss me. Not until tomorrow perhaps." Her head drooped as though too heavy for her neck to support. She propped it up wearily with her right arm. Then listless, she stood up from the table like a sleepwalker, having eaten only half a bowl of oatmeal. "You risked your life for me."

"That's my job," he said.

He was the lighthouse keeper. Rescuing those who ventured upon the sea was his vocation and his calling. And perhaps somehow it was also his penitence for those innocent enemy soldiers he had killed during the war. Faces floated in his mind: the young first lieutenant he had shot in the chest whose blue eyes had grown wide in astonishment at the approach of Death; an older soldier who had spit up blood when Jeremy stabbed his bayonet into his abdomen. The first, someone's son; the second, someone's husband.

"I'm no hero," he said.

She reached her hand forward tentatively to touch him again, but he withdrew.

"I'm still very tired," she said.

"Ya sleep in the bedchamber," he told her. "I'll bunk down here by the stove. I've been up most of the night."

Guided by an inner map, she returned to the bedroom. Not until she closed the door did he hear her crying, heart-wrenching sobs in mourning for her father.

Almost immediately, he fell asleep, and the nightmares began. Artillery fire. Booming cannons. Screams of agony. Blood. Death. Shells screeched across the sky. The frightened faces of men and boys illuminated by the red explosions. Arms and legs scattered over the green field. Horses stumbling, falling. He screamed out in his sleep. A smooth hand soothed his forehead. His eyes opened, and an angel with auburn hair hovered over him. Was he dreaming still? A hand stroked his smooth cheek and then the scarred one tentatively. He waited to see if she would draw back her hand in horror, but she didn't.

Nevertheless, he recoiled from her touch.

"What frightens you so?" she asked.

"Nothing," he answered gruffly, reluctant to let her into his life.

"Last night, you braved the ocean when I was sure the tide would pull me under."

He did not answer.

"My father said you were a soldier in the war. It must have been awful. Is that what haunts you?"

*What did she know of the horrors? She who had been sheltered and protected all her life. Who would protect her now?*

He fought down a sudden impulse to draw her face to his and kiss her. Passion he'd thought long dead welled within him and made his stomach taut.

But her blind eyes saw nothing. He could not take unfair advantage.

"I feel like I've known you a long time from listening to my father talk about you and from holding your carvings."

He kept her at arm's length, swallowed hard, and muttered, "I'll fix supper."

"Let me," she said. "I'm not helpless, you know. Do you have any eggs?"

He stood and fetched the eggs as well as a cast iron skillet.

"They're gulls' eggs," he said. "I found them in the dunes a few days ago."

She smiled weakly and took in the shape of them

with her hands. "Show me where you keep the salt and pepper."

When he handed her the shakers, she sniffed them to distinguish one from the other. She deftly cracked the eggs and scrambled them up with a spatula.

"In Ireland, my mother always chopped up potatoes in the eggs."

"Ireland," she repeated. "That explains your melodic way of speaking."

They ate in awkward silence interrupted only by Bailey's begging. The mantel clock struck five.

"I have ta go ta the lantern room ta work now," Jeremy said.

"I'll wash the dishes."

Jeremy climbed the stairs with a bucket of oil to refuel the lamp. From the top of the tower, he looked out at the dark ocean heaving and sighing below. The clouds had cleared. The pale sun lit the white caps below.

"Oh Marion, are you somewhere in those inky depths?" he whispered.

## Chapter Three

During the night, Jeremy drank hot, black coffee to stay awake. His eyes blinked heavily, and his head kept nodding forward, jolting him back to attention. At dawn after extinguishing the light and cleaning soot from the lantern and windows, he descended the stairs and lay on a quilt spread on the floor by the potbellied stove. As far as he knew, Abigail still slept. He awoke mid-afternoon and found her feeding Bailey scraps of beef on bones.

"We didn't mean to startle you," she apologized.

"No, I need ta get up. I have things ta do, and tomorrow we need ta see about takin' ya back ta the main land. Right now, what I need is a bath."

"I'll heat some water," she said.

Jeremy noted that she'd become quite familiar with the layout of the kitchen and moved about with ease. She quickly retrieved a pot and pumped water at the sink. Jeremy dragged a copper tub across the floor to the bedroom.

"No need to be modest," she said. "I can't see a thing."

Jeremy blushed.

They filled the tub alternating hot and cold water, then Abigail gave him his privacy.

"Don't empty the tub," she said. "I'll wash some clothes later."

\*\*\*\*

While Jeremy bathed, Abigail returned to the kitchen where she found onions and browned them in a skillet with melted butter before turning them into a pot of salty water.

The bedroom door creaked open.

"What smells so good?"

"Onion soup."

"I'm really hungry."

"I baked bread earlier." She cut him a thick slice and slathered it with butter. "Tell me about Ireland."

"So it's Ireland ya'd like ta hear about. Sad story that. 'Tis a thousand shades of green—fields and pastures and wilderness dotted with sheep and Border collies and winding roads. The coast is like it is here, rocky and treacherous. Tha cottages have thatched roofs, tha old castles are crumblin', and tha people are starvin'."

"But surely there are farms and fishing."

"The potato famine," he explained. "The English own most all the land. Poachers are shot or arrested by the lairds who sit on their arses and grow fat off the rents. Pardon me speech. I don't speak like this ta a lady, but the beauty and the sadness of Ireland makes ya want ta weep."

The lyrical quality of his voice mesmerized her and made the story more poignant. "Would you ever go back?"

"I might one day if I ever have money enough ta buy land or a shop. The soup was good. Ya're a fine cook."

"Thank you." She stood and moved before the fireplace holding her hands out toward the flames to warm them. "Papa said there were other carvings."

"In front of ya on the mantel."

She lifted her hands and tapped around the shelf. The first item she brought down felt like two hands brought together in prayer. She could even feel indentations where the fingernails were located. Next, she brought down a cross where a man hung in agony.

"I tried ta carve a crucifix from memory."

There were other statues of Bailey and one of a Madonna with a child.

"I want ta send that one ta my mam for Christmas."

The last one was tall and thin with a circular rail. "Is this the lighthouse?" she asked.

"'Tis."

"Would you take me up to the top?"

He hesitated. "Only if ya promise never ta go up alone. It wouldn't be safe."

"I promise."

He led her to the stairs and placed her right hand on the rail. "The stairs spiral upward," he explained.

When they reached the top, he let her feel the unlit lamp and gripped her arm tightly as they stepped onto the parapet. A strong ocean breeze blew their hair back from their faces. Abigail's eyes shone with exhilaration.

"I wish I could see out over the waves. It must seem like flying. Are there any stars yet?" she asked.

"One or two. They look like distant fires—Jesus, Joseph, and Mary!" he exclaimed. "A shooting star. It just blazed across the sky. I wish ya could 'ave seen it."

Her face lit up over his excitement. She rested her small hand on top of his on the railing and electricity shot up his arm.

"You're cold." He removed his coat to wrap

around her. "We'd better go back down." He let his arm linger protectively across her shoulders as they descended. "I have to go back and light the lamp."

"You'll need this," she said at the bottom of the stairs. She removed his coat and gave it back to him.

As they parted, Jeremy fought the overwhelming urge to kiss her soft pink lips. He ascended the stairs in a happy daze. He remembered her beautiful profile in the light of the setting sun—her flawless complexion and thick and black lashes. He had suppressed an urge to reach out and stroke her soft, unblemished cheek.

His hands trembled as he lit the wicks because he wondered what it would be like to place his hands around Abbey's slender body and draw her close to him. Would it scare the daylights out of her? Would she reach up touch the horrible scar and draw back?

*I'm an idiot. I took this job because I wouldn't have to be around people. I know that no one wants a man who looks like a monster. If she could see me, she'd have gone home at the very first chance.*

He kicked the iron stair rail in frustration.

*I promised myself I'd never get involved again, never put myself in a positon where I'd experience rejection and heartache.*

The sea murmured outside. The lonely wind howled.

*Mam always said if you made a wish on a falling star it would come true. But that's just Irish superstition like leprechauns and fairies. We're hopeless dreamers the lot of us.*

\*\*\*\*

While Jeremy manned the tower, Abigail poured more hot water into the copper tub, located a bar of soap, and took a bath, washing her long hair and ridding her body of salty residue. When she finished, she dried off and took one of Jeremy's flannel shirts from the wardrobe. Then she put her own clothes and his dirty clothes in the tub and washed them. Finally, she wrung them out and hung them near the bedroom fireplace. Then she sat before the smoldering embers combing and drying her hair. It fell in long, soft waves across her shoulders, no longer matted and stringy.

*Nothing awaits me at home but an empty house.*

Swallowing back the sob that rose in her throat, she blinked back tears.

*Aunt Agatha will expect me to move in with her. But I'm not a child. Oh no, the cat! I forgot all about him. He must be starving by now. I have to go home soon, but I don't want to leave. I want to stay here with Jeremy.*

\*\*\*\*

"If I'm going to stay awake, I've got to get coffee," Jeremy told Bailey who looked up approvingly. The dog followed him back down the stairs where he filled a cup with lukewarm coffee.

"I don't care how I drink it. It's the extra energy if gives me."

Jeremy stopped in his tracks. Candlelight seeped under the door of the bedroom. *Abbey must have fallen asleep without extinguishing the candle.* He opened the door. She sat in a chair with his shirt coming down to midthigh revealing her shapely calves, slender ankles, and dainty bare feet.

He swallowed hard. He'd not seen a female's legs since the days he and his younger sister had jumped together in the bog sinking up to their thighs in the viscous detritus.

"Bailey? Is that you?" she asked.

"I didn't mean to disturb ya privacy." He backed up.

"Jeremy?" she asked turning red. "I hope you don't mind that I borrowed a shirt. My clothes were so dirty."

"No, no, of course not."

"My own should be dry by morning."

"I'll leave ya then." He withdrew and shut the door. He leaned back against it. If he'd been half an hour earlier, he'd have caught her bathing. He pictured the soap gliding over her slender, ivory neck and soft breasts and groaned softly.

*Get ahold of yourself, lad. You'll be needing a priest for confession of lustful thoughts.*

Chapter Four

As the sun slipped over the horizon the next morning, Jeremy stared at his disfigured face reflected in the lighthouse window. It was like being splashed with a bucket of cold water, a jolt into reality that Abigail had made him temporarily forget. He extinguished the lamp and went for a walk along the shore in the growing light of dawn. The sun colored the clouds orange and yellow ochre. The waves played a sort of rhythmic melody like an Irish ballad.

He needed space to examine his feelings. When he'd put on his coat and faced the bracing air, he'd left Bailey at home to watch over Abigail. He intended to circle the entire island.

The very thought of Abigail made his heart race, but she didn't understand his life, his self-imposed exile. She didn't know that strangers and children turned away from him in fear and horror. They cringed at the sight of his face scarred by a fire that had swept through his tent when a shell had ignited a keg of gunpowder nearby. His left ear had been nearly burned off, and the pain had been excruciating. He wore his wavy hair long to cover the abnormality.

He'd been bitter after the war especially after he'd sent the boat passage so his sister in Wexford, Ireland, could travel to America and then had received the letter from his parents about her passing. The job on the island had taken him away from the wide-eyed stares and gaping mouths of strangers who gawked when they saw him for the first time. But nightmares still haunted him.

Cold air filled his lungs and made him more alert. Splintered boards and the bow of a small boat lay beached on the sand. He quickened his pace and reached the wreckage. Clearly, it was the remains of Marion's boat. Only the bow was still intact, and he found an airtight tin lodged in the corner. He opened it and discovered the cranberry scones. They smelled delicious, and he bit into one. He could not help but devour it. Replacing the lid, he continued his jog.

The storm surge had cast seaweed and algae over the rocks and beach. It gave off a faint fishy smell that attracted the gulls. They screeched and hollered at each other in their relentless search for food.

*What did Marion tell her about me? Does she just feel sorry for me? I don't need anyone's pity.*

His increased pace had brought him full circle faster than he'd anticipated, but questions continued to circle in his mind. When he finally entered the house, Abbey sat by the fireplace.

"I found ya father's wrecked boat," he said. "I believe these are yours." He handed her the tin.

She opened it, smelled the scones, and lightly touched them. "They were a gift for you."

"For me?"

"Yes, to thank you for the wood carvings."

"That was nothing."

"To me, it was everything. It helped me to know, to understand, to see animals, their shapes, to touch the creatures of the world."

"Well, thank ya for the scones."

An awkward silence followed.

"We really should get ya home today," he said finally. "People will think I've kidnapped ya or worse. Ya need ta plan a memorial service for ya da."

"I don't want to go back yet," she said. "The house will be so empty, so lonely without him." She coughed slightly, and air seemed the rattle in her chest.

He felt her hot, clammy forehead. "Are ya all right, then? Sometimes, people develop pneumonia when they've had water in their lungs."

"I'm fine. And I want you to sleep in the bed today while I do some sweeping and dusting. You need some real sleep. I know I have to go home soon. I just can't face it all now. Will you come with me to plan the funeral, I mean? You said he was your best friend."

"I don't think it's a good idea."

"Because of the scar?" she asked.

*How did she know?* She touched it, he remembered, but she hadn't drawn back.

"It doesn't matter to me. It shouldn't matter to anyone," she insisted. "What's important is what's in the heart. Please go get some sleep. Your voice sounds weary."

Jeremy obeyed like a contrite wee lad scolded by his mam. This time when he settled back on the pillows and drowsed, he did not dream of artillery fire and death. He dreamed of Abigail lying in his arms and wearing his flannel shirt.

\*\*\*\*

Abbey swept and mopped the kitchen. She chopped more onions, tomatoes, carrots, and some of the whiting Jeremy had caught in his net the previous day. Her father had always liked her fish stew. At the thought of him, she had to wipe tears from her eyes with the back of her hands. Bailey looked concerned and whimpered. She sat down, and he laid his massive head in her lap while she rubbed his silky ebony ears.

*You'll be fine, Abbey girl. That's what Papa always said.*

She felt Bailey's collar and wrapped the fingers of her right hand tightly around it.

"Take me for a walk, boy," she said as she stood. She took one of Jeremy's coats down from a peg on the wall and then, holding onto the dog, ambled outside. The roar of the surf told her the ocean had not calmed significantly. She hadn't said anything to Jeremy about her fear of crossing the ocean again. She shivered as she remembered the undertow snatching her under like a ravenous beast.

The dog pulled her along as he sniffed at various objects. Abigail reached down to feel what he had located. She touched the five spindly arms of a starfish and felt the raised bumps on its surface. The harsh cry of gulls rasped overhead.

Suddenly, Bailey bolted loose. Abigail stood and experienced a moment of short-lived panic. "Bailey?" she shouted.

The dog bounded back. She reached down and found a stick in his mouth.

"You want to play?"

She took the stick and threw it, hurling it through the salty air. Bailey's paws drummed against the sand as he chased after it and then proudly trotted back with his toy. They played for nearly fifteen minutes until Abigail's arm grew tired. Then she secured a grasp on

Bailey's collar.

"Home, boy," she commanded. She sighed as she thought of her father, and she swallowed back rising sorrow. A hollow emptiness filled her chest.

Bailey instinctively knew she needed his assistance. He walked slowly and steadily.

\*\*\*\*

The striking of the clock roused Jeremy at one in the afternoon. Stretching his arms above his head, he'd not felt so relaxed in weeks. The outside door opened, and he leapt from the four-post bed. Bailey and Abigail entered the house along with a puff of cold air.

"Ya went outside alone?" His voice was shrill to his own ears.

"No," she said. "Bailey was with me. We've been playing fetch."

Somewhat mollified, he rummaged around the kitchen.

"I made something special," Abigail said. She took the lid off the pot of fish stew slowly simmering on the stove and added more salt and pepper.

The low rumble of thunder sounded outside. A flash of lightning lit up the kitchen.

"Looks like we won't be going ta Arbor today," Jeremy said from the window.

Rain drummed against the panes in a steady rhythm as they ate the chunky stew.

"Papa said he brought you *A Tale of Two Cities.* It's one of my favorites," Abbey said.

"He read it to ya?"

"Oh no, I read it myself," she answered proudly.

"But how?" Jeremy's eyebrows drew together in bewilderment.

"Don't be so amazed. I read Braille books. Papa ordered them from Boston."

"I don't understand." Jeremy was mystified.

"Do you have paper and a pencil?"

Jeremy retrieved some from a desk drawer where he kept his records and log for the Light Keeping Service. Abigail put the paper on top of the table and pressed the pencil down hard. Then she lifted it and turned the paper over. She let Jeremy feel the raised dot.

"This is the letter *A* in Braille." Next she punched in a colon. "This is the letter *B*. Two dots side by side is *C*."

"Amazing. I never knew. It's sort of like Morse code. Write the entire alphabet for me," he said with enthusiasm.

"I will if you read aloud to me while I work."

Jeremy took the Dicken's novel down from the mantel. "I'm up to the part where Madame de Farge is knitting her infamous list."

"The names of all the aristocrats she wants punished," Abigail said.

"Yes, heads will roll, as they say. I understand. I know what it's like ta be hungry. It gnaws at ya. It make ya desperate, desperate enough ta board a coffin ship and cross an ocean ta a country where ya know no one."

"A coffin ship?"

"More passengers in steerage are buried at sea than make it to shore. I was lucky not ta be seasick like so many others. But I digress."

He began to read about Dr. Manette cobbling shoes. His voice was melodic, animated, and expressive in his effort to entertain her.

"You read well," she said when he'd finished the chapter. "I can see it in my mind. Papa took me to a play once with actors who had memorized their parts. He would tell me what they were doing on the stage. When it was over, he took me up to feel the curtains and the trap door in the floor."

"The Irish are wonderful storytellers," Jeremy said. "And they like ta sing ballads. The sadder and more maudlin, the better."

He replaced the leather book on the mantel and came to watch her progress on the alphabet. As he looked over her shoulder, goosebumps prickled her skin. Jeremy traced the dots on the paper with his forefinger.

"This is hard. I have too many callouses. I can't tell one set of dots from another."

Abigail reached out to touch his hand to confirm what he'd said. The tips of his fingers were thick and rough.

"I play the fiddle," he explained. "Rather badly, I'm afraid. Sometimes Bailey howls."

Abigail laughed. "I want to hear you."

"No, ya don't. Take me word for it."

"Please," she implored.

"Maybe later. Right now there's work ta do, and ya're going ta help me."

He led her up the winding stairs of the tower to the lantern room.

"I have ta trim the wicks. They float on these small platforms in the oil. Can you feel where the tops are black and burned?"

"Yes."

"You take the scissors and trim them. I'm going to clean the smoke residue from the windows."

"Tell me more about the coffin ships," she said.

"Ya don't want ta hear about that," he warned. "'Tis depressing."

"Yes, I do."

"You're sure?"

She nodded.

"The stench in steerage from tha waste buckets is unbearable, tha moans of those suffering from seasickness and from cholera unsettling. Rats with wild eyes and skinny tails scurry about sniffing for any crumb, chewing through the ropes, spreading fleas and disease. Sometimes, tha whole ship shudders like a great, wounded beast about ta descend into a murky grave. The winds howl like a banshee during storms. We were fortunate ta have a priest on board ta help us pray and give last rites over the dying."

"How awful," Abigail said.

"Course, above on the deck were the accommodations for the wealthy passengers, lairds and ladies who had private cabins, who ate with the captain and first mate, and played cards in the smoking lounge."

"How many of the passengers in steerage died?"

"Ten to fifteen Irish a week. Of course, they were half-starved when they boarded, and many of them already sick. They were tossed overboard to be swallowed by the waves as the rest of us led by Father Mulvaney prayed our Hail Marys and Our Fathers for them."

When the work was completed, Abigail persuaded Jeremy to play some music. "We need some cheerful tunes to raise our spirits," she insisted. "Papa always said that music feeds the soul."

Jeremy got the fiddle down from the top of the walnut wardrobe with the brass knob. "It's turbly out of tune," he said as he turned the pegs and plucked the strings. Then he rosined the bow.

"Say that again," Abigail said.

"What?"

"Turbly." She imitated his Irish accent.

"I'll have none of ya teasing." He positioned the fiddle under his chin and ran the bow over the strings playing a lively reel. Bailey romped around as though dancing and, true to Jeremy's prediction, began to howl along.

"It's lovely," Abigail said, clapping in time to the music.

"Wait a minute," Jeremy said. He put down the violin and went into the bedroom. He returned with an instrument that resembled a tambourine but was slightly larger. It had a thick wooden stick to beat on it like a drum.

"'Tis a bodhran." He handed it to Abigail. "Instead of clapping, keep rhythm with this."

Abigail practiced for a few moments and soon created her own syncopated beat. She couldn't see the grin on Jeremy's face, but she felt the warmth of his approval.

Later, alone in the bedroom, Abbey couldn't sleep. She knew her time on the island was drawing to a close, and she could think of nothing but Jeremy—his lyrical voice, his gentle touch, his radiating charm.

*Does he feel anything for me?*

She turned over and tried to get comfortable. She

punched the feather pillow and smoothed out the quilt. Tomorrow, she would be going back to an empty house, an empty life.

\*\*\*\*

The retreating storm clouds scurried across the face of the full moon. Jeremy sat mesmerized by the reflection of moonlight on the heaving ocean, the curling waves, and the white seafoam. He wanted nothing more than to climb down the stairs, get in the bed with Abigail, and wrap his arms around her, never to let her go. But she had to go. The people in Arbor would be worrying, wondering what had happened to her and to Marion. She would go back to her life in Arbor and forget all about him.

The next morning, he awoke to rattling pots and pans. When he descended the stairs, she was baking biscuits in a Dutch oven next to the fireplace. As she turned to face him, the hem of her dress swept into the dancing yellow flames.

"Abigail, you're too close to the fire!" He sprinted to her side, overturning a chair in the process, and tackled her to the floor. He beat out the fire with his bare hands. He straddled her breathless and afraid until he realized that the danger had passed. The warmth of her body pressed against him. He stood up and then helped her to her feet as well.

"Did I hurt you?" He inspected her looking for signs of damage.

"No." Gently, she took his hand and placed it palm down right above the hollow between her breasts. A faint quiver fluttered like the wings of a bird beating against its cage.

"Whenever I'm near you, my heart races," she said.

He encircled her slender waist and drew her to him. He kissed her, and she kissed him back, wrapping her arms around his neck.

"I think I'm falling in love with you," she murmured.

His mouth moved to her neck. He lifted her in his arms and was about to carry her to his bed when he thought about his sister, of the way his parents had always protected her from men with selfish intentions. He put Abbey back on her feet.

"I love ya more than words can say," he said in a voice husky with emotion. "I know it may seem impulsive, but I want ya ta be my wife. Will ya marry me, Abbey?"

"I feel we're married already, joined spirit and soul. I want to be with you every day of the rest of our lives." She laced her fingers through his.

Suddenly, he knew that her place was with him, that somehow Marion or the sea or God had brought his Abigail to him.

"I'm serious," he said in a low voice. "You'd best give it some long thought. 'Tis not something to take lightly."

"I'm serious too," she said. "We'll arrange matters when we go back to Arbor."

He gently kissed her forehead. "Let me finish tending the biscuits," he said. "I don't want you near the fireplace again before I buy a screen."

"Is my skirt beyond repair?" she asked, turning around.

"It's black as soot about a foot in height and two feet wide. And still smoking a bit."

"It will have to do until I go home."

Jeremy had a fleeting image of her in his flannel shirt again as he grabbed a pot holder, took the handle of the Dutch oven, and moved it to the table.

Abbey hummed one of the lilting Irish tunes Jeremy had played the previous night as she put water on the stove to make coffee. Then she retrieved the coffee grinder and ground the fragrant beans.

"The day is clear, and the ocean is calm," he announced. "I'll take you back today and send someone out to light the lamp tonight. After your father's funeral, we'll borrow a buggy and ride to Augusta. We'll find a priest or a minister and get married."

"I love you, Jeremy McKetcheon," she repeated. "Abigail McKetcheon sounds good, doesn't it?"

"Like music." He kissed her, and their lips lingered.

Abigail put a canning jar of blueberry jam on the table along with mugs of steaming coffee. Jeremy removed the biscuits and slathered one with churned butter. Then he slid a note into her hand.

She gingerly fingered the paper. A smile spread slowly across her face. "You wrote: I love you, Abbey, in Braille."

Whimpering, Bailey padded into the room and sniffed around Abbey's singed hem. The dog knew something was going on. After coffee and oatmeal, Jeremy packed food and water for their trip and stored the provisions in his boat.

He pushed the dinghy to the edge of the sea and helped Abigail aboard. He tucked a wool blanket around her to keep her as warm as possible. As the next wave washed up, he shoved off and called Bailey to jump on, and then boarded himself. Securing the oars in the oarlocks, he rowed easily out toward the ocean while Bailey lay down with his head in Abigail's lap. Abbey clung to both sides of the boat so tightly her knuckles turned white.

"The sea is calm today." He tried to ease her fears. "The incoming tide is in our favor and should make our trip easier and faster."

But Abbey did not loosen her grip. Plovers flew overhead, and to starboard, a whale breached, then fell back into the ocean, slapping the water with its flukes.

"Ya wouldn't believe it," he cried to Abbey. "A humpback whale!"

Her face turned ashen.

"No, there's nothin' to be afraid of," Jeremy hurried to explain. "It's not close, and they don't eat humans. They strain tiny organisms from the surface of the sea."

"It won't—it won't turn the boat over?" she asked.

"Nay, she's headed out to the deep water and migrating south."

"You'll have to carve one, so I know what it looks like."

Chapter Five

"Something must be wrong," Agatha insisted as she paced the kitchen. "I talked to the other fisherman, and they said Marion and Abigail left three days ago. They should be back by now."

"The weather has been abominable. They might have decided to stay on the island until the storm passed." Jack calmed his wife.

"I think you should send someone out to Lighthouse Island. Marion is getting too old to be rowing out there with the mail and groceries. I hear the keeper is a young man. He should come into town himself and fetch his own supplies."

"Agatha, it's an important job that young man does out there guiding ships along the coast. Marion just tries to be helpful."

"Please talk to some of the lobstermen, someone with a boat, and send them out there."

"I'll go myself," Jack said.

"No," Agatha replied. "You shouldn't strain your heart. Send one of the younger men over."

\*\*\*\*

"I can see the wharf at Arbor," Jeremy reported. With his right hand, he shielded his face from the sun. The golden orb beamed down on them, and only a few clouds cast shadows across the landscape, the rocky coast and the evergreen forest of tall conifers. The brown fields of the farms lay fallow after the harvest. The deciduous trees blazed in autumn reds, golds, and yellows. To starboard, a pelican dropped from the sky and dove into the water in search of fish. Seaweed and kelp floated in the water as they drew closer to shore.

"I see some otters bobbing on their backs," Jeremy narrated. Bailey began to bark. "Quiet down." Jeremy soothed him.

"Let me help you row," Abigail offered. "Papa taught me how. He said it would build muscle."

"I'm fine," he said, subduing a small laugh and continued on. Abbey might be many things, but muscular wasn't one of them.

After half an hour, he told her he could make out the farmhouses up on a hill.

"Do you see the one with a red barn?" she asked.

"Yes."

"That's my aunt and uncle's farm," she answered. "Jack and Agatha Thompson. They raise chickens and a few hogs. I dread telling them about Papa. Agatha is his older sister."

Jeremy pulled harder against the oars. He wanted to reach the mainland before the tide turned. As they approached the docks, several fishing trawlers headed out. One of the fishermen on the wharf, Isaiah Stone, recognized Jeremy and hailed him.

"That's McKetcheon from Lighthouse Island," he told the others. "Help him tie up."

Jeremy cast his lines toward them, and Isaiah pulled the dinghy to the moorings. Bailey jumped out first, rocking the boat, but Jeremy steadied Abigail and assisted her ashore.

"Abigail Morrison," Isaiah said. "The whole town

has been worried. Where's Marion?"

Jeremy glanced at Abigail, and when she remained quiet, he answered for her. "Marion's boat broke up against the rocks. He went down. I'm afraid I wasn't able to save him."

"My God, he drowned? I'm sorry to hear it. When?"

"Three days ago, but I haven't been able to bring Ab—Miss Morrison back due to the storm."

"The sea is a treacherous mistress," Isaiah said.

"Please don't tell my aunt and uncle until I have a chance to speak with them myself," Abigail said.

"Aye, we won't," said several of the fishermen gathered around them.

"I'm sorry for your loss, miss," said a lobsterman, Richard Hart, whose ruddy complexion was as red as a boiled lobster. His weathered skin was tough as leather.

"Isaiah, could you possibly go to the island and man the light tonight? I'll return tomorrow to relieve you. I need to see Miss Morrison home."

"I'd be glad to help you," Isaiah said. He looked at the young keeper and then at the blind daughter of his old friend.

Abigail put her arm through Jeremy's and explained how to get to her street.

"I'd say those two might be sweet on each other," Richard noted when they were out of ear shot.

"Don't go poking your nose where it doesn't belong," Isaiah said. "Help me relaunch this craft."

\*\*\*\*

Abigail climbed the rickety porch steps and tried the brass knob. "It's locked, and Papa would have had the key." She bit her lower lip.

"Stay here. I'll see if any of the windows are ajar," Jeremy said.

He moved around the gray clapboard cottage, trying each black shuttered window as he went. He found the kitchen window open about six inches, pushed it up with effort, and hoisted himself inside. Then he unlocked the front door. Abbey and Bailey entered. The dog immediately began sniffing around and checking out the main room, his thick tail wagging like a metronome. But Abbey teared up.

"I can smell his pipe and tobacco just like he's still here." She broke down.

Jeremy wrapped his sinewy arms around her and drew her close.

"I wish I could have saved him, Abbey. I'm so sorry. I miss him too."

She swiped the tears away. "I know you do. And I know you did everything possible." She stood on tiptoe and kissed him. "I need a handkerchief."

Jeremy pulled a clean, white, folded handkerchief from his back pocket. Abbey dabbed her eyes and got her emotions under control. "You always seem to have whatever I need," she murmured in reference to the handkerchief.

Jeremy swept her hair back gently from her forehead. "I'll always try ta have whatever ya need."

"Oh my goodness. I wonder where the cat has gone?" she asked suddenly.

"You have a cat?"

"Yes, an orange tabby. I'm afraid I forgot all about him with Papa and everything. Here, kitty, kitty." She clucked.

"I suspect he went out the window to find food."

"Of course, poor Charlie. I wonder if my aunt and uncle have fed the chickens."

Before they could look for Charlie, an urgent series of knocks sounded at the front door. Abigail opened it, and her aunt and uncle swept into the house like a nor'easter.

"Abigail! How I've worried." Agatha embraced her niece. Over Abbey's shoulder, she caught sight of Jeremy and sucked in her breath. He turned away embarrassed.

"Who are you?" she demanded.

He stepped forward. "Please allow me ta introduce myself. I'm Jeremy McKetcheon, the light keeper out on Lighthouse Island."

"Yes, I recognize you," Uncle Jack said, but Agatha just stared, her mouth agape.

"So, child, where is your father?" she asked finally.

"Aunt Aggie, Uncle Jack, please sit down."

"Is he upstairs?" Agatha asked, sinking down in the gooseneck rocker by the fire.

"Papa and I went out to the island three days ago. We were caught in that raging storm. Our boat hit the rocks, and we were thrown out."

"What!" Her aunt gasped. "I knew something had happened. I just knew it."

"Jeremy and Bailey saved me, but—Papa was lost."

"Dear God." Agatha's hand came up to her chest. Uncle Jack, who still stood, walked up behind her and put his hands on her shoulders in a comforting gesture of reassurance. "He's gone? My little brother, the last living member of my family, is gone?"

Jeremy again felt his inadequacy as Agatha wept

quietly.

"I knew it. I felt it in my bones."

Laconically, Uncle Jack stroked his chin with his hand and stared down at the floor.

"We must plan a memorial service for him," Abbey said, kneeling down in front of her aunt.

"And his body?" Jack asked.

"It was not recovered," Jeremy said. "I dove for him again and again. The undertow was tremendous. I blame myself. I counted him as my greatest friend here in Arbor."

As though recovering her senses, Agatha rose from her seat and pulled Abbey to her. "My child, my child, you will live with me and your uncle now. I know that Marion's will names us as your guardians until you come of age."

"Auntie, I'm not a child," Abigail said.

"Of course not. But you're not yet eighteen."

"No, but I'm engaged," Abigail explained.

"Engaged? When? To whom?"

"We are going ta Augusta ta wed as soon as possible," Jeremy said. "We'll leave immediately after Marion's memorial service on Friday."

Agatha turned to Jeremy. "I can't believe you! You took advantage of a blind girl whose father died? What kind of man are you?"

"Aggie, calm down," Uncle Jack said. His eyes pled with Jeremy's for understanding. "My wife's had quite a shock today."

"I've taken advantage of no one," Jeremy said. His jaw formed a hard line. "We could not return before taday; the water was too uncertain."

"Of course, you couldn't," Jack said.

"He saved my life! Not once, but twice!" Abbey defended Jeremy. "And I love him. I love him! And he loves me."

Uncle Jack walked up to Jeremy. "We thank you for saving our niece," he said. "Agatha, we will go home now, and they will join us for dinner tonight at six o'clock. We insist. And then they will spend the night with us."

"But—" Agatha said.

"We'll see you at six o'clock," Uncle Jack reiterated firmly.

"Yes," said Abigail with hesitation.

"Good-bye then." Uncle Jack pecked her cheek and ushered Agatha outside.

"That did not go well," Abigail said after they'd left.

"No," Jeremy agreed.

They heard Bailey barking in the kitchen, and a cat yowling at the window sill. Charlie had returned.

Jeremy grabbed Bailey and pulled him into the other room, as Abigail took the frightened tom in her arms and soothed him before pouring him a saucer of milk. She smelled it first to make sure it had not soured.

"Abbey, how old are ya?"

"Seventeen," she answered.

"When do ya turn eighteen?"

"In October."

"Then ya are too young. I had no idea."

"Too young for what?"

"Ta marry without parental consent."

\*\*\*\*

"What do we know about him?" Agatha complained as she fried chicken in a cast-iron skillet.

"He may be after her inheritance."

"She hasn't much of an inheritance," Jack said. "The house is mortgaged."

"He's an uneducated immigrant."

"He fought for the Union," Jack said, "and was wounded. Marion spoke highly of him. And he's got a decent job."

"No doubt, he's a Catholic as well," Agatha complained, barely listening to her husband.

"It's the same God, Aggie, and the same Jesus Christ."

"There's a school in Boston with an excellent reputation, the Pearson Academy for the Blind. You know I've been after Marion for years to let her go there. She could probably even teach."

"She could stay with us," Jack countered.

"No, it's too close. They could run away together. Please, let's send her to the academy for a year. She'll be with people like herself, people who understand her limitations. She'll be protected—not on some island with no doctor, no one at all except that horrid fellow."

"The man was injured fighting in the war that preserved this nation. I know that Marion liked and admired him."

"But Abigail can do better, and what if they should have children? How could a blind girl watch after children on an island in the middle of the treacherous sea with no one to help her? They're young and unrealistic. She's confusing gratitude with love."

Jack studied his wife. Agatha's feet were firmly planted, and her chin tilted upward in that maddeningly stubborn way she had when refusing to alter her opinions.

"How are you going to convince her?"

"I'll take her on a trip to Boston. In a year, if they have not forgotten each other, we'll see about their seriousness."

Agatha had made up her mind. Jack sighed, knowing from experience that further debate would be useless.

"She is too young," Agatha reiterated.

"She's not too young to know her own mind," Jack warned.

****

By quarter to six, Abbey had changed into a cranberry-colored dress that brought a blush of red to her cheeks. Jeremy had never seen a woman more beautiful. Conscious of her aunt's disapproval of him, he'd used Marion's razor and carefully shaved the stubble from his face and tried to subdue the unruly curls of his hair with a comb.

Abigail felt his smooth cheek and smiled. He'd noted that she touched the left cheek and wondered why she avoided the scarred right one. *Does it matter to her? Or did she do it out of deference because of my tendency to draw away?*

"I love your curly hair," she said, playing with the soft waves. "Mine is so straight."

"Ya aunt doesn't like me."

"Give her time. Aunt Agatha never likes anyone the first time she meets them, but she's really not so awful. It's cold out," Abbey said. "Wrap one of Papa's scarves around your neck."

He acquiesced, and they set out for the Thompson farm. Bailey tried to follow, but Jeremy commanded him to lie down on the porch. He whined a little but obeyed.

"Your aunt does not seem like the type who easily changes her mind," Jeremy said as he led Abbey up the street.

"She will when she gets to know you better."

"Mommy! What's wrong with that man?" A little girl pointed from across the street. Jeremy stiffened.

"Hush!" her mother reprimanded and hurried her away. If Abbey had heard, she said nothing.

The climb to the farm was steeply uphill, and the cold wind chilled their faces. When they reached the front porch, Uncle Jack opened the solid wood door. He'd been watching for their arrival like a nervous rooster. "Come in, come in."

"Do I smell fried chicken?" Abbey asked. "Aunt Aggie, you fixed my favorite."

*Why did I not know fried chicken is her favorite meal?* Jeremy rarely had a chance to eat chicken on the island.

The farmhouse was cozy inside with the lamps lit and a fire burning on the hearth. Red and white gingham curtains hung at the windows and matched the tablecloth on the dining table. Jeremy pulled out a chair for Abbey and then took a seat himself. At the head of the table, Uncle Jack said grace. Agatha passed a basket of hot buttermilk biscuits around, followed by a pot of cranberry jam, then heaping bowls of mashed potatoes and boiled kale.

In spite of the hospitality, Jeremy sensed tension. Could Abigail feel it as well?

"I think Papa would have liked a simple memorial," Abbey said. "We will ask his friends to gather in the parlor of the house on Friday. I'll play his favorite hymns, and Uncle Jack, will you please choose some Bible verses and give the eulogy?"

Jeremy had noticed the mahogany spinet piano at Abigail's house but had not realized that she played.

"He liked 'Amazing Grace,' " Aggie said.

"And 'The Old Rugged Cross,' " Jack chorused.

"I still can't take it in," Agatha said. "I keep thinking that he's going to walk in the door." She sighed.

Jeremy was keenly aware they considered him an outsider. He remembered sitting at his own kitchen table with Marion and sharing a cup of coffee or hot tea. Their gradual friendship had grown beyond discussing the weather, yet Marion had never told him about his daughter's inability to see.

Conversation continued to revolve around plans for the memorial and then took a turn, a non sequitur.

"Of course, the two of you will stay here tonight," Agatha said. "I've already planned a big breakfast. Abbey, you can have the upstairs bedroom, and Jeremy can have the downstairs one. We don't need rumors of impropriety."

"I agree," said Jeremy, seeing his chance to win Aggie's goodwill. "I have ta return ta work tomorrow but will be back for the memorial Friday."

When he saw Agatha rise to gather their empty plates, he rose as well. "Let me do the dishes," he offered.

"I'll dry," Abigail volunteered.

"I'm sorry about my aunt," she whispered when they were alone in the kitchen and then stood on tiptoe to kiss him. "She doesn't understand."

He kissed her back a bit desperately, somehow

afraid they were losing their grasp on one another. "I'll miss ya until Friday," he said in a husky voice.

Chapter Six

The next morning, Jeremy smelled good pork sausages sizzling in the kitchen. He stretched, got out of bed, and dressed. He missed Bailey's nosey interference. Female voices rose in the dining room.

"Abigail, you can't marry that man. He had no business keeping you on that godforsaken island for three days. His appearance is frightful, and how could you ever have children living on an island and you unable to see? They would be in constant danger of drowning."

"Aunt Aggie, with all due respect, it is not your decision to make!" Abbey's voice was resolute, almost rude.

"You are my only niece, and my brother so recently in his watery grave. You must come live with me and Uncle Jack. We'll rent out Marion's house if we can."

"I am going to marry Jeremy. He saved my life not once but twice, and I love him."

"And I love her," Jeremy said, emerging from the hallway. "She'll be well protected and cared for, I assure you."

He recognized a look of astonishment and embarrassment at being overheard as it crossed Agatha's face.

"Mrs. Thompson, I have no wish ta offend ya. I

had hoped ta be accepted inta the clan, but I will not give her up. I've a steady job and decent pay. And I'd never put her in harm's way." He swallowed hard.

"What's all the noise about?" Uncle Jack came down the stairs.

"Nothing," Agatha said with tight lips that meant *everything*.

They ate breakfast in silence except for a few attempts by Jack to lighten the mood. Afterward, Abigail gathered the dishes and took them to the sink. She returned and gave Jeremy an extra sausage. "A treat for Bailey," she said and kissed him on the cheek.

"I wish I didn't have ta go back taday," he said.

"Your job is important. The ships can't navigate safely without you. I know I have to share you with all those sea captains. But you come back on Friday. Remember I'll be waiting for you."

Jeremy took his frustration out on the oars of Isaiah's boat as he and Bailey moved over the choppy surf back toward Lighthouse Island. A few lobstermen checked their pots and carefully removed the large greenish-brown crustaceans. A dory or two headed out to fish. The wind had picked up and cut through his wool jacket like an icy blade.

An hour and a half later, he pulled the dinghy up beyond the rocks and returned to the house to relieve Isaiah Stone.

"Don't know how you do it night after night," Stone said. "I kept falling asleep, but every time I woke up the lamp was burning. It's kind of spooky out here at night, with the light casting long shadows on the floor and the wind howling like a ghost."

"I can't thank ya enough," Jeremy said. "If ya will

give me just a minute, I want ta write a letter ta the Light Keeping Services headquarters and request a temporary assistant. Abigail and I are going ta Augusta ta be married Friday after Marion's service."

"Congratulations!" Stone said, slapping him on the back. "She's a fine girl, a fine girl."

"I want ya ta carry the letter back and post it for me," Jeremy explained. He hurried to his desk, scratched out the missive, and sealed it in an envelope.

Stone tucked it inside his jacket and set off in his own boat. Jeremy waved at him as he got out beyond the breakers.

When he and Bailey returned to the house, the cottage seemed lonely and empty without Abbey. Even the soft sea breeze whispered her name. Jeremy sat on his bed, despondent. What if Agatha was correct? What if Abigail grew unhappy with the isolation of the island? There was no way to move her piano from the mainland. Would she one day regret her decision? He got up and looked in the small wall mirror at his lopsided face, something he usually avoided. Then he pulled it from the wall and dashed it to the floor, splintering glass over the pine boards.

His mother had always called him her darlin' boy when he was young. She hadn't seen him since the war. He had downplayed his injuries so she wouldn't worry. He wondered what she would think of him if she saw him now.

****

Abigail returned to her own house at noon. She fed Charlie, scratched him behind the ears, and set him out on the porch. Then she crossed the street to buy some staples and ask Myrtle to spread the news about the memorial service for her father.

"I will surely get the information out," Myrtle said. "Poor child, it must have been dreadful staying on the island with that wretched man."

"That wretched man saved my life," Abigail said. "He tried to save Papa as well. I don't know how Jeremy stood that cold water so long."

"Oh," Myrtle said, realizing her mistake. "I'm sure he was very brave."

Abigail gathered her supplies and left. *Does everyone in this town just judge people by their looks?* Abbey stormed across the street, entered the house, and slammed the door behind her.

She'd not been sitting long with her knitting before a rap sounded at the window. She was finishing the green scarf first intended for her father and now intended for Jeremy.

"Who is it?" she called out.

"Aunt Aggie."

Abbey sighed, put the yarn aside, and unlocked and opened the door.

"I've come to make peace, and I hope you will forgive me," Agatha said. "I know something as unimportant as Jeremy's appearance means nothing to you. You must realize that so much has changed in such a short time that I am quite beside myself."

Abigail softened. "If you would give him a chance and get to know him, you'd see for yourself how wonderful he is."

"Yes," Agatha said. "More time is needed. We do agree on that. I wondered though if you would make one last trip as a single woman with me to Boston. I know how you loved the theater, and you could find a wedding dress there."

"I haven't thought much about a dress," Abbey said. "When you can't see, it hardly matters what you wear. I know most of my dresses by the number and shape of the buttons, the texture of the cloth, and the feel of the collars."

"We could travel by train and shorten the time," Agatha said. "You'll need a veil, of course."

"Oh, all right, if it means that much to you," Abigail said. "You know, Auntie, you only see the disadvantages of Jeremy's life, but I am no proper wife myself. I know my sightlessness is a burden in many ways. Jeremy is patient. He is kind. Many men would never think of marrying a blind woman."

"Oh, Abigail, if you could only see what a beautiful girl you are. Any man would be proud to have such a lovely wife."

"I would like to buy him a wedding band," Abbey said. "I still have my mother's, and that is the one I want to wear."

\*\*\*\*

To expend some energy, Jeremy walked swiftly around the island in spite of the bracing air. He found one smooth gray-blue bit of drift wood among detritus tossed up by the waves. Though he doubted Abbey had ever heard of such a thing, he remembered a tradition in Wales where men carved love spoons for their betrotheds. He rubbed the wood with sand to smooth it some more and jogged back to the house.

Traditional love spoons were carved with hearts, diamonds, and other symbols. Jeremy fashioned one with a heart in the handle, but then added a bird in flight soaring over the ocean. He hoped that Abigail would like it.

Later, he blindfolded himself in an experiment to see what it was like in Abigail's world. Bailey barked suspiciously at his changed appearance. As his master located a broom and dustpan, the dog backed up and continued to yelp. Jeremy fumbled his way into the bedroom and swept up the mess he'd made of the mirror. Though tempted to look at the results, he instead felt around the floor and cut himself on one of the shards. Leaping up to rinse the abrasion, he bumped into the rocking chair and tripped over one of the rockers.

Frustrated, he pulled off the blindfold and bound his finger with it. He realized how important it was for each piece of furniture to remain precisely where it was. One could not leave buckets or, in the case of children, toys lying about haphazardly. One must be careful to return pots and dishes to their rightful storage spots.

*How much we sighted people take for granted.*

Recognizing him once again, Bailey bounded up, placed his front paws on Jeremy's chest, and licked his face.

*How had Abbey maneuvered the house so well?*

Each night, he kept the light burning and went about his usual chores, but he was no longer content alone upon the island that had become his sanctuary after the war. He now yearned to be near Abbey. She was never far from his thoughts. They were together in spirit if not in person. The Friday memorial service seemed an eternity away. He went outside to walk the island. Seagulls screeched and fought each other over dead creatures in the detritus washed up by the ocean. They circled and dive bombed.

Suddenly, Jeremy saw vultures circling, circling over the corpses of fallen soldiers, some dressed in blue Union uniforms, others in Confederate gray. He shook his head to erase the images of the vanquished 63rd regiment, his comrades and his friends. Instead, he would focus on Abigail, his gift from God.

Chapter Seven

Abbey sat at the piano, her tapered fingers moving over the ivory keys, playing "Sweet Hour of Prayer." Most of the family's friends and neighbors had gathered and given their condolences, but to her knowledge, Jeremy had not yet arrived. Had he changed his mind? Or worse, had his boat been overturned in the ocean like Marion's?

Who would save the light keeper?

Her uncle left his spot next to her on the piano bench and stood to address everyone as she finished the last line of the hymn.

"We have gathered here today to honor our own, my brother-in-law who was as close as a true brother. Marion Morrison was the type of man who was there when you needed him. He loved his God, and he loved his family. He always had a smile and funny anecdote to lighten your day. He will be sorely missed."

Aunt Aggie wept softly as she sat on the sofa and blew her nose into her handkerchief. Then Abigail recognized the familiar Irish accent as Jeremy whispered to her aunt, "Aye, he was a good man."

Abbey turned her head in his direction as her uncle continued.

"One text that Marion always quoted was from the Gospels, 'In my father's house, there are many mansions. I go to prepare a place for you.' Marion has gone home to the Father, and one day we will go home too. 'Weep not as those who have no hope,' the apostle Paul wrote. 'The angels in heaven today are rejoicing over the death of one of the saints.' "

Abbey heard Isaiah Stone rise, and her hands roamed over the piano to accompany him as he sang "How Great Thou Art" in a rumbling bass baritone. The service ended with the Lord's Prayer.

Mourners mingled with one another in the crowded house and ate the food they'd brought to the family: oyster pies, fish stews, pot roasts, chicken, and vegetables. Vanilla cakes and fruit pies with flaky crusts lined the sideboard as well.

Jeremy's arms wrapped around Abbey in a warm hug. "Sorry I was late," he said. "The tide was against us all the way. I hope it's all right I've left Bailey tied ta a post behind the house. God knows, I hope he doesn't start ta howl like a banshee."

Agatha presided over the beverages offering tea, coffee, and apple cider. She was pleased to overhear stories about her brother from friends and neighbors.

"Sorry for your loss," Mary Weaver told Abbey.

Jeremy led her to a less crowded corner and found her a seat. "You never told me you could play the piano so well. Won't you miss it?" he asked.

"Not as much as I've missed you." She squeezed his calloused hand.

"There's a tradition in Wales," he said, "where a man carves a love spoon for his bride ta be. I made one for ya this week."

He handed her the carefully crafted piece of wood and watched delight glow in her eyes as her long, sensitive fingers traced each groove.

"I thought perhaps you had changed your mind," she said.

"I don't change easily, Abbey," he said, "especially when someone is as important ta me as yourself. We can leave tomorrow for Augusta. I have a replacement at the lighthouse for two weeks."

"Don't be upset with me," she said as a preface. "I made a compromise with Auntie. She is taking me by train to Boston for a day or two to buy a wedding dress and have one last trip together. I'll be back no later than Monday night. And you and I will leave Tuesday."

His silence made her anxious. How she wished she could see his face. "I'm sure Uncle Jack will let us borrow the team and wagon for our trip. You and Bailey can stay here at the house. Go through some of Papa's clothes and see what you might want. Give the rest to Mrs. Stapleton. I don't think I can stand to go through his belongings."

"I won't say I'm not disappointed," Jeremy said at last. "But we do have the rest of our lives together."

"I'm going to buy your wedding ring in Boston," Abbey said. "And I have Momma's ring that you can put on my finger. It's a simple gold band with a single pearl. I know exactly where Papa kept it."

\*\*\*\*

Tumultuous feelings blocked Jeremy from peaceful sleep. Agatha had whisked her niece back to the farm and left him to bed down at Marion's. A strong undertow had ripped him from Abigail and swept him away in an opposing current. Bailey sensed his restlessness and wandered into the room whining.

"Come here," Jeremy called. The dog jumped on the bed and lay on top of the blanket. Soon warm and pacified, he fell asleep long before his master. Bailey's faint snoring and slightly whistling nose were comforting.

Sliding from beneath the covers, Jeremy padded in stocking feet to the fireplace and stared into the dying embers. The red orange glow cast an eerie haze around the room and elongated his shadow. Slowly the embers died out, and he couldn't help wondering if Abbey's love for him would do the same. He found himself quietly praying that God would not take her out of his life.

\*\*\*\*

Before she was even fully alert, Abbey found herself on a buckboard bumping along the rutted road from Arbor to the train station in Portland. Her uncle had tucked a thick, wool blanket around her, but her nose was numb and cold. A knitted hat kept her ears warm, and a cable-knit scarf encircled her slender neck.

She had no idea what clothes her aunt had packed in the carpetbags in the back of the wagon. She knew only that they would stay at the Harbor Inn near the Boston common and see *My American Cousin* at the Boston Players Theater. Abraham Lincoln had watched the same play the night of his assassination.

Abbey could hear the *clip-clop* of the horses' hooves, the jangling of the reins, and the drumming of the wooden wheels. She smelled Uncle Jack's pipe and the fresh pine-scented air.

"I'll be back to pick you up at the station Monday morning at nine o'clock," Uncle Jack said. "I've got to look after the farm."

"What type of ring do you think I should buy Jeremy?" Abigail asked. "I think gold is better than silver. It doesn't tarnish. We measured his finger. He should wear a size eight."

"Gold is better especially in our moist salty air," Uncle Jack agreed.

Agatha shot him a disapproving look as if to say, don't encourage her.

It took forty-five minutes to reach Portland. When they arrived at the depot, Jack jumped down and grasped Abigail around the waist to help her to the ground. She'd brought a cane to tap back and forth in front of her. Her aging aunt huffed and puffed as she also descended from the rickety wagon with her husband's dutiful assistance.

Uncle Jack unloaded their luggage, mounted the platform, and paid for their train tickets. Abbey heard the murmured conversations of other travelers.

"The locomotive should be pulling in within the next fifteen minutes," the ticket attendant said. "You can wait on that wooden bench over there."

Abigail took her aunt's arm, and they made their way across the platform. Soon, a chugging engine and a sharp whistle roared through the trees.

"You both be very careful," Uncle Jack said. He kissed Abigail on the cheek and hugged his wife.

The two women entered the open-air passenger car to the sound of the hissing locomotive. Abigail counted the number of seats they passed, so she would know how to find her place again on the left side of the car.

"The ones here in the middle look good," Agatha said. "And we'll be warmer."

The padded seats were much more comfortable to Abigail's bottom than the hard wagon seat or the bench. She heard other passengers boarding as well as the sharp cry of a hungry baby. All the hustle and bustle was a bit disconcerting. She was glad when everyone found their seats, and the train departed to the sound of rumbling iron wheels and clanging brass bells.

Soon, in spite of the incessant *clackity-clack* of the wheels, Abbey closed her eyes to avoid the sting of cinders and smoke. And then she dozed. She dreamed of Jeremy and Bailey and her time on the island. At noon, her aunt awakened her.

"Let's go to the dining car and order some lunch," Aggie suggested.

Abigail held onto her aunt's hand and trailed behind her as they switched cars. It was warmer in the enclosed, dark paneled carriage, and Agatha ordered hot chamomile tea and ham sandwiches.

"These are delicious," Abbey said when their order arrived and she bit into the ham on rye. She munched contentedly and ordered a refill of tea. "How old were you when you married Uncle Jack?" she asked her aunt.

"Me? Oh, I was twenty-five, a bit spinsterish," Agatha said, "but I wanted to take it slow and be sure I married the right man."

"And then you lost the two babies," Abbey said. "Papa told me."

"Yes, miscarriages both at about three months," Aggie said. "One a girl, the other a boy."

"And later?"

"I just never conceived again," Agatha said. "We gave up on the idea of becoming parents. But then your mother had you, and Marion was so kind to share you with us. No one knew about your blindness, not for months. You were such a happy infant. It wasn't until you started crawling around bumping into things and crying when you heard someone's voice."

"Do you think I might have a blind child?" Abbey asked.

"I don't know," Agatha responded. "There are blind people with sighted children."

"Oh, I'm not feeling sorry for myself," Abbey said. "It's just that a blind wife and a blind child might be a huge burden for a man."

"You'd need help," Agatha agreed.

"You know, Auntie, I've never actually cared about not seeing because I can smell and feel and hear things, such lovely things like music, but I would like to see Jeremy, his kind eyes, his gentle mouth."

Agatha cringed a little. She couldn't help it, and for the first time, she imagined the pain the man must have endured in acquiring his hideous badge of courage.

"Is he really so disfigured?"

Agatha paused. "You can tell he was once a handsome man, Abbey. He's medium height, strong and slender. His hair is dark and wavy, and the left side of his face is rugged and handsome enough, a firm jaw, nice profile."

"And the right side?"

"It's red and wrinkled. His ear, I'm afraid, is quite mangled. He's fortunate he did not lose sight in his right eye."

Abigail nodded, lost in thought. "The pain must have been excruciating," she said, remembering how he had saved her from the fire.

"Child, I know you think I'm meddlesome and controlling, but you mustn't confuse sympathy and pity with love."

"Oh, I don't," Abbey said quickly. "He's loving

and brave, talented and artistic. He's reliable, and he makes me feel...alive."

"He's a bit rough around the edges," Agatha said. "I understand he's not had the benefit of an educated and refined upbringing. I'm not being a snob. I just want the best for you."

"He can read and write, and he's learning Braille. He's a gentleman in every way that counts!"

Her raised voice engendered glances from other passengers.

"Hush, child," Agatha hissed. "Don't speak so loudly. We're in public."

"We have made sacred promises to each other in God's eyes," Abbey said in a lower voice.

"I've not seen the man at a Christian gathering since he arrived in Arbor."

"There's no Catholic Church in Arbor. We don't even have a Protestant one with a building."

"I don't want to argue."

"He has a crucifix in his house. I felt it, and I felt the suffering of Christ as never before."

"Please don't get overexcited. I'm sure he's fine in his own way.

"He's fine in every way."

Agatha sighed wearily. "What do you know of his family, child?"

"His parents are renting land from an English landlord outside of Wexford. They're farmers like us, but the potato blight has caused heavy losses. Hundreds are starving. His older brother Shawn is caring for the parents. Jeremy came here to work and raise passage for his sister, Bridget, to come over, but she died in Ireland while he was fighting in the war."

"Those are his only siblings?"

"Yes."

"Well, one always hears that the Irish have broods of children. Taking care of so many children is quite a task and hard on a woman."

"You don't think I can handle being a mother?"

"I did not say that. Let's not spoil our trip arguing."

"I am already married in heart, mind, and soul," Abigail insisted.

Chapter Eight

On the island, Jeremy stirred a bucket of whitewash to begin painting the tower. As a day marker, it had to make a sharp contrast to the sky. Bailey trotted behind him wherever he went, his tail high in the air. Though the morning was crisp, the day promised to be a sunny one. The round yellow orb took the edge off the chilly air.

Jeremy worked steadily for hours and then gave in to Bailey's desire to play fetch. They ambled along the shore, as Jeremy tossed a stick out into the waves for the dog to retrieve.

*I'm an island man through and through, first Ireland and now Lighthouse Island.* He looked out to sea at the churning ocean, the blue heaving surf. He couldn't help but consider Aunt Agatha's reservations. *Will I be able ta protect Abbey alone on the island?*

Had it been Providence or blind good fortune that he'd been in the house when her dress had caught fire? What if he had not been in the house? What if they did have children? Would she be able to handle motherhood? He knew in Ireland even sighted mothers sometimes had children stumble into the fireplace and become singed or worse. On the island, the added danger of the capricious ocean loomed as a hazard.

But Bailey could help. Maybe they'd get a Border collie as well, and he could make a pen for the child to play inside. He'd once gone to sea to fish with his uncle in Ireland and been tied round the waist by a loop with the rope secured to the mast in case he fell overboard. They would just have to be cautious, careful, and prudent.

He felt better and then caught sight of his face reflected in a tide pool left behind by the retreating ocean. Would his own child be horrified by his awful face? He shuddered and prayed it would not be so.

\*\*\*\*

The B & L locomotive had pulled into the Boston station at the corner of Causeway and Andover Streets. Abbey marveled as her aunt explained they'd crossed the first movable bridge built in America, one that spanned the Charles River. The screech of the halting wheels and an exhalation of hissing steam sounded like a gigantic snake. Her aunt stood and offered Abbey an arm. They departed the train with Abbey using her cane to tap back and forth the space in front of her.

Aunt Agatha hailed a hansom cab, and they climbed inside. A uniformed footman stored their luggage at the rear.

"The Harbor Inn," Agatha told the driver. A whip snapped, and the cab lurched forward.

"We just passed Faneuil Hall where the Declaration of Independence was once read aloud to the patriots of Boston," Agatha said. "In the common, a few lazy cows are nosing the frosted grass for edible vegetation. In the distance are the tall masts of whaling ships, frigates, and clipper ships in the choppy, gray harbor."

The cab stopped, and the footman helped them alight and retrieve their bags. After checking into their room, the women peeled out of their winter wraps.

"A lovely four-post bed with an eiderdown quilt," Aunt Aggie said with appreciate. "Some very fine stitches."

Abigail felt the soft coverlet.

"A colorful maple leaf pattern. Pretty autumn hues, browns, russets, and muted yellows."

Abigail didn't tell her that colors really meant nothing to her.

Agatha poured water from a china pitcher to the basin and wiped her face with a cool cloth. "We must divest ourselves of the grime of travel."

She wiped Abbey's face clean and then brushed out her niece's hair before rebinding it in a bun at the nape of her neck.

"I'm a bit tired," Aggie said. "Let's nap and then have a meal sent up to the room before we leave for the theater."

Abbey readily agreed and lay down on her side in the comfortable bed with her aunt beside her. Soon the older woman snored loudly, then Abbey dozed as well. When they awoke, they ordered a hearty beef stew.

"I like the celery in it," Abbey said. "The gravy is good too. It's been a while since I had carrots."

"Boston has ships arriving daily from all over the world," her aunt said. "Perhaps they're from South America. But we must hurry and dress for the theater. I brought your cranberry-colored gown. We can walk to the theater. It's right down the street, and the street lanterns will illuminate our way.

"I'm wearing that olive green gown with the black velvet trim on the sleeves. The one you helped me sew last fall. Can you help me pin this cameo at the neckline?"

Abbey moved toward her aunt's voice, took the pin, and attached it to the material.

At the theater, an usher led them to their seats in an upper balcony, but they could hear well, and Aunt Agatha assured Abbey that she could see everything fine. "I'll whisper all about it to you when the play starts."

The play revolved around an American who traveled to England to claim his inheritance. The most comical character, Lord Dundreary, always mixed up proverbial sayings like "Birds of a feather gather no moss." Abigail laughed. She joined enthusiastically in the standing ovation at the end.

"That was quite pleasant," Agatha said. "It's been years since I've seen a play. I used to imagine myself a bit of an actress."

"Really, Auntie?" But as she thought about it, Abbey realized her aunt did have a flair for the dramatic.

"Oh, I played a role or two in school skits, but that was all long, long ago."

"I don't think I'd be able to remember all the lines," Abigail said.

The next morning she arose before her aunt and nudged her awake. "I want to shop for a wedding band after breakfast," Abbey said, swinging her legs over the side of the bed.

"There's one place we need to visit first," Agatha replied.

"Where?"

"That's my little secret. You'll find out soon enough."

Abigail had no choice but to follow. The streets in Boston were so much livelier than Arbor. Pedestrians engaged in animated conversations. She heard the movement of numerous carriages and the cries of street vendors hawking various wares. They traveled several streets from the inn before Aunt Agatha led Abbey up a set of entrance stairs.

"Where are we?" Abbey asked.

"We're at the Pearson Academy for the Blind," Agatha said. "Most of the students live here, and they're taught Braille, sewing, musical instruments, all sorts of things."

"Why are we here?" Abbey stood still, her feet planted in rebellion.

"You'll find out in just a moment," Agatha coaxed. Her aunt addressed a woman presumably at a front reception area. "We have an appointment with Matron Bards," Agatha said briskly.

"Yes, she is expecting you?" a lower, feminine voice said.

"Why do we have an appointment?" Abbey asked, but they were whisked into an office.

"You must be Mrs. Thompson, and this must be Abigail."

Abbey felt a cool hand shake her own. Puzzled, she sat in the chair offered to her.

"Abigail, your aunt wrote me about what a talented girl you are. I understand that you read Braille, play the piano, and are very good with children."

"Ye—yes."

"We have an opening for a teacher here at Pearson. It includes room and board as well as twenty-five dollars a month. Our children range in age from six to fifteen. Some have been blind from birth; others have been injured in accidents or lost their sight due to diseases such as scarlet fever."

"I don't understand what that has to do with me," Abigail said. "I'm about to get married."

"I can't tell you how difficult it is to find good teachers," Matron Bards continued. "So few people truly understand the needs of the blind, and some of the children who were born sighted suffer from depression due to their loss of vision. Qualified people are few and far between. Your aunt just wanted me to take you for a tour of the school."

"Of course, I will tour the school, but as I said, I am about to be married." Abbey's tone of voice remained adamant.

"If you will both follow me," Matron Bards said. She took Abbey's arm and tucked it into her own.

"The first room we'll visit is our music room," she said. "The strings class is practicing now. We have violin, viola, and cello."

As they entered, Abigail heard a metronome ticking, and someone conducting. "Once again from the beginning, with more feeling this time."

Several stringed instruments played a tune that she recognized as "The Battle Hymn of the Republic."

Continuing down the hall, they visited the sewing room, where the pedals of sewing machines whirred.

"I've always wondered about sewing machines," Abbey said, interested in spite of herself.

"Caroline, will you please let our guest check out your machine?"

Abbey heard a childish voice say, "Yes, ma'am." She pictured a little girl with soft curls.

"This is the wheel that makes the needle go up and down when I work the pedal," the girl explained. "Be careful about the needle here." She led Abigail's hand to the sharp point. "Feel the groove in the plate beneath the fabric. That's how we guide the garment so that the seam is straight."

"How old are you, Caroline?" Abbey asked.

"Twelve."

"And what are you making?"

"A shift, sort of an undergarment or nightgown with a drawstring around the waist. We sell them to help fund the academy."

"That's lovely," Abigail said, feeling the soft muslin.

Then they went into a classroom, where Abbey heard the masculine voice of a teacher lecturing on American history. He explained about the first battle of the Revolutionary War at Lexington and Concord calling it "the shot heard round the world."

"It seems you have a wonderful school here," Abbey told Matron Bards. "If I had known about it a few years ago, I might have attended."

"I tried to get your father to let you come here," Aunt Agatha said.

"I didn't know that."

"I am going to take you to our sitting room where you can talk," Matron Bards said. "I'll return after a while." They continued down the corridor.

"Abbey, come sit on the sofa with me," Aunt Agatha said with a deep sigh. "You need to know that you cannot marry at the age of seventeen in the state of Maine without the consent of your parents."

"But I have no parents."

"No, but your father's will made you our ward, myself and your uncle Jack."

"What is your point?" Abigail stood and paced the room.

"We feel that working here at the Pearson Academy would give you ten months to consider this life-changing decision."

"Ten months!"

"If both you and Jeremy still want to marry at that time, you will do so with our blessing."

"Ten months!" Abigail repeated.

"There is so much good you could do here, and you would learn new things yourself. You would gain experience that might come in handy if you should ever be widowed and need a job. Abigail, please be reasonable. Jeremy has a dangerous job, and your uncle and I are also up in years."

"Does Jeremy know about this?"

"He will be told," Agatha said firmly.

"No, you just want to discourage him." Abigail threw up her arms.

"If he truly loves you, he will wait," Aunt Aggie insisted.

"But he does love me."

"Then he can be patient for a few months."

"A few months. It's almost a year."

"And this is the first man you have ever courted," Agatha argued.

"What does that matter?"

"You are probably not the first woman he has courted."

"You tricked me," Abbey said. "This is the real reason you wanted to come to Boston."

"I am trying to honor your father and do what is best for you." Agatha broke down into tears. Abigail softened a bit and tried to put herself in her aunt's place.

"Oh Auntie, you still think of me as a child, and I am not a child!"

"You'll always be our little girl. And you can save up some money that could pay off the mortgage on your father's house. If we can find a tenant, it will be rented out while you are away. But few people are moving to Arbor. Even though Jeremy is employed, it never hurts to have more than one source of income. Believe me, I know. The years when our crops have failed or the chickens have gotten ill have been difficult. Life has numerous uncertainties."

"Do you swear to me as a Christian that you will deliver a letter to Jeremy from me?" Abigail said. "And that if I am unhappy, you will bring me home sooner than ten months?"

"Yes," Agatha said, "and maybe Jeremy can come visit you."

"You have not been forthright with me," Abigail said. "I'm angry with you, and I wonder if I can even truly trust you."

"You can," Agatha said. "And after we tell Matron Bards your decision, we will go buy Jeremy's ring and see about having a wedding dress made for you."

"A dress that I won't wear for almost a year?"

Chapter Nine

Jeremy found that few of Marion's clothes fit him. The pants were too short, the sleeves too tight. He felt funny going through the man's personal belongings, but Abbey had asked him to take care of her father's possessions. They smelled of Marion's aromatic pipe tobacco, and Jeremy missed him. He folded the shirts and trousers neatly and took them across the street to Arbor's one store.

"Hopefully, someone will get good use out of them," Mrs. Stapleton said.

A small boy pulled on his mother's skirt and asked for a piece of candy. When Jeremy turned around, the lad stared with gaped mouth.

"Here," Jeremy said, pulling a shiny copper penny from his coat pocket. "I had a sugar tooth when I was a lad."

The child took the penny but continued to stare.

"Tell him, thank you," his mother reprimanded.

"Thank you," the boy murmured as he looked down at his own scuffed shoes.

Jeremy returned to the empty, cheerless house and sank down into the gooseneck rocker. Outside, the wind howled, and a hazy mist blew in from the Atlantic.

*Oh, Abbey girl, I miss you. I want ta go back ta our island, love.*

\*\*\*\*

True to her word, Agatha took Abigail to a dressmaker whose shop was down the street from the house that had once belonged to the silversmith Paul Revere. Betsy March and one of her assistants measured Abigail.

"Of course, we're terribly busy with Christmas coming and so many orders for party gowns. But we could start on the dress, the first of next year."

She showed Agatha various dresses in the fashion tableaus, which Agatha described to Abbey the best she could.

"Your niece has such beautiful blue eyes. I think a white dress with blue trim would be quite lovely on her," Mrs. March suggested brightly. She held the material up against Abbey's ivory complexion.

"Yes, that's perfect," Agatha agreed.

"I don't want anything so fancy it can't be worn again," Abbey said.

When they'd made a final selection on the pattern, they left the dressmaker and walked down the street to the goldsmith's shop.

"I would like something unique," Abbey said.

"Tell me a bit about your husband to be," the jeweler said.

"He's a lighthouse keeper."

"Hmm. A lighthouse keeper. There's a ring that is different in this case. Was made for a sailor. The outside of the band is in a pattern that looks like the coils of rope, but the inside where it touches the skin is smooth."

He took Abbey's hand and placed the ring in her palm. She liked the heft of it.

"Size eight?" she asked.

"Yes, and you could have something special engraved on the inside."

"This one is perfect."

\*\*\*\*

On Sunday afternoon, Jeremy and Bailey walked up to the Thompson farm. Deciduous trees blazed with reds and golds, and squirrels chattered to each other from the branches. A low silvery mist lay on the ocean, and the smell of the sea permeated the air. Near the russet barn, Jack Thompson mended the fence with a ballpeen hammer in his right hand and nails in the pockets of his overalls.

"Could you use some help?" Jeremy asked.

Bailey sniffed along the ground.

"I'm almost done," Jack said, pounding another nail into a board.

"I wondered if I might accompany ya ta meet the women tomorrow at the Portland Depot?"

Jack stood up straight and proceeded cautiously. "That would be fine. But I think I'd best warn you. There was another reason that Agatha took Abigail to Boston."

"I'm listening."

"Agatha and I have nothing against you, nothing at all. But we feel Abigail is a bit young, and as we are her legal guardians, we want to give her a chance to acquire further education and experience if she wants it. The trip to Boston was not just for pleasure."

"Why didn't Abbey tell me this?" Jeremy asked.

"She didn't know."

"Ya tricked her?"

"We are not objecting to the marriage, if both of you are still willing when she turns eighteen October

12."

"That's nearly a year away!"

"Ten months," Jack said.

"Abbey'll never agree. She'll return on that train unless Agatha forces her ta stay. Have you sent her ta a school?"

"She's to be employed."

"But I can take care of her," Jeremy protested.

"Her father left little money, and the house is mortgaged."

"How much is owed?"

"Twelve hundred."

Jeremy gave a low whistle. "My salary is fifty dollars a month, but I live rent free. Why not sell Marion's house?"

"Who would buy it?" Jack asked. "The town is so small, and more people are leaving than staying. The winters here are so harsh. We'll be lucky if we can rent it. Abigail told us you send money home to your parents."

"'Tis true, but I've also money in savings. I've been frugal ta a fault."

"Abbey will be earning a wage for the first time in her life. I'd offer to help pay off the house myself, but other than the eggs we sell locally and the blueberries and cranberries we ship to Boston, we don't make much ourselves. I inherited the farm from my parents."

Jeremy sighed. "Money always seems ta be a problem. Still, I'd like ta go ta the station. I'm sure Abbey will return." But even as he said it, a stab of fear hit him in the pit of his stomach. *What if she doesn't return? What if she's changed her mind?*

\*\*\*\*

Abbey sat up in bed and fingered the gold wedding band she'd bought for Jeremy and now wore on a filigree chain round her slender neck. Aunt Agatha had left to return to Arbor, and Abigail was having second thoughts about not leaving with her. Still, she wanted peace in the family.

She sighed, got out of her narrow bed, and dressed. She'd been given a tiny room beneath the sloping roof of the refinished attic where several of the teachers boarded. It was small but sufficient with a wardrobe, pitcher and basin, a chamber pot, and a small dormer window. A rap at the door startled her, and she opened it.

"I want you to work with the elementary Braille class today. You'll have three students: Lucy Watkins, Jimmy Barnes, and Everett Dyches. Lucy is eight and like you blind from birth. Jimmy is ten and had scarlet fever two years ago which took his sight. Everett, well, Everett has some behavior problems. He is deaf as well as blind."

"Blind and deaf," Abbey said, sad for him because he'd never hear music or birds chirping or dogs barking or a human voice. In a sudden revelation, she surmised that people probably felt the same pity for her about her lack of sight.

"He knows a bit of sign language," Matron Bards said. "Make a fist with your right hand. Now, feel my fist with your left hand." She assisted Abbey. "Pretend my fist is a head. If I move from the wrist up and down, I mean yes. If I bring my fingers out and snap them down on my thumb, it means no. Everett recognizes this."

"He must feel very locked up in his own world,"

Abigail said.

"He's very angry and frustrated at times," Matron agreed. "Sometimes he throws fits or lashes out at other children." She led Abigail down the hall twenty feet. Abigail had already learned to turn right and reach for the stair rail. There were twelve steps to the second floor, then a short right turn, and twelve more steps to the ground floor.

"Now turn left, and you will feel the classroom door on the right. Miss Ida Allen will be with you in the classroom. The door is locked during class time so the children cannot leave the room and wander off unattended. But here is your key."

Matron put a ribbon around Abbey's neck with a brass key dangling from the middle. Abbey felt it with her sensitive fingers.

"We have a new teacher here today," Miss Allen said as they entered. "Say hello to Miss Morrison."

Two voices chorused, "Hello, Miss Morrison."

"She is blind too, but she can read very well, and she is going to help you learn Braille."

To Abbey, she said, "When we work with Everett, I will sign the alphabet letter into his right hand as you let him touch the Braille equivalent with his left."

\*\*\*\*

Jeremy had cleaned Marion's house, washed the dishes, and swept the front porch. He'd planned a breakfast of oatmeal, and the porridge simmered on the stove. He removed the pot and let the stove cool. Then he dressed and shaved, anticipating the feel of Abbey in his arms.

"Sorry, but you have ta stay here," he told Bailey.

The dog whined but allowed himself to be tied to

the porch rail.

As Jeremy walked to the Thompson farm, the air was crisp, but the sun shone, and the sky radiated a brilliant blue. Jeremy found himself whistling in pleasant anticipation. Tomorrow, he would be a married man. He and Abigail would borrow the Thompson's wagon and ride to Augusta.

Next to the red barn, Jack had hitched the horses, two bay mares, to the carriage for the trip to the Portland.

"Nice day for a buggy ride," he said when he saw Jeremy. "Climb on up."

Jeremy sat on the right side of the rickety seat. "Bailey wasn't too happy about being left behind, but a train station is no place for a dog, 'tis sure."

"Indeed not," said Jack. He climbed aboard, settled himself, and gave the reins a snap. The wagon lurched forward. "You ever been to Portland?"

"Came through on my way ta Arbor. I know there's a lighthouse there."

"Yep. Rugged coastal town, a bit larger than Arbor, and they do have a restaurant and an inn, couple of churches and two schools. The railroad is helping it grow."

\*\*\*\*

Abigail found Lucy and Jimmy to be quick learners, but Everett only communicated with grunts and yelps that were sometimes ear-splitting. He didn't seem to enjoy having both teachers working with him at once. He sniffed Abigail and touched her face.

"Maybe we should encourage him with treats," Abbey suggested.

Suddenly, Everett let out a piercing scream and

rolled back and forth on the floor. The noises frightened Lucy and Jimmy. Abbey wrapped her arms around the blind and deaf boy, cradling him gently and rocking him back and forth until he calmed down.

"Go look in my room," she told Miss Allen. "Take Lucy and Jimmy with you. On the table by my bed, you will find a carved spoon. Please bring it to me."

When Miss Allen returned with the Welsh love spoon, Abbey moved Everett's index finger inside the heart and spelled heart into his hand. Then she put his hand palm down over his own heart and let him feel the vibrations. She repeated this sequence several times and then let him touch her lips as she carefully enunciated *heart*.

"H, h, h, h," Everett said.

Abbey put his hand over her fist and nodded. "Yes! Yes!"

\*\*\*\*

Late that afternoon as the horses clip-clopped over the bridge to Portland, Jeremy took in the size of the city. There were numerous shops, a bank on Middle Street with a tall clock tower, a small white Presbyterian church, and Molly's Restaurant. While Main Street in Arbor was just about the only street, Portland had numerous thoroughfares and short alleys. He caught sight of the Portland lighthouse standing tall on the rocky shore. It was taller with more outbuildings than the one he serviced in Arbor.

Men, women, and children milled about Portland Station. Some carried satchels as they prepared to board. Others, like he and Jack, looked as though they planned to meet passengers.

They heard the train before they saw it. The sharp

whistle and clanging bells announced its approach, and then the puffing locomotive emerged from the forest with steam belching from its sides.

Jeremy filled with anticipation jumped down from the wagon, but his emotions deflated when he watched Agatha step down from one of the passenger carriages alone.

He swallowed down his disappointment though tears stung his eyes. He blinked to control them. "All this soot," he said to Jack, quickly swiping his eyes with the back of his hands.

They approached Agatha who grimaced when she saw Jeremy. "I didn't expect you," she said.

"No, ya did not. I hope I haven't startled ya." He waited for an explanation.

"Abigail's feelings for you are unchanged," she assured him. "But I hope you understand why Jack and I made this decision."

"I understand, but I do not agree," Jeremy said. "Ten months or ten years will not change my feelings. But I cannot speak for her."

"She sent you this." Agatha pulled the sealed envelope with Abigail's note from her fabric purse.

Chapter Ten

Jeremy's heart sank. Physically, it was as if a giant, knuckled fist had struck his abdomen. Politely, he took the note from Agatha. "I'll read it when I'm back in Arbor." He slipped it into his shirt pocket.

Then he helped Jack collect Agatha's bags and put them in the back of the carriage. On the ride home, he only half listened to Agatha's chatter about Boston, the shops, the theater, the play.

*Abigail, why have ya done this ta us?*

When he was finally alone at Marion's house, he pulled out the letter and opened it.

*Dearest Jeremy,*

*I miss you already, and I hope you will not be too disappointed in me. My aunt and uncle refused to give permission for our marriage until my eighteenth birthday. And I do not want to cause a terrible rift in the family. I'm wearing your future wedding ring on a chain around my neck to keep you close. I hope you will get a chance to visit me as you will always be in my thoughts. I am at the Pearson Academy for the Blind in Boston.*

*My love always,*
*Abigail*

He had not realized she could write in cursive and surmised she had used a ruler to keep the lines straight, though some of them sloped. In one spot, the ink was blotted by a drop of water. *A tear?*

*Ten months! It will be the longest ten months of my life.*

He returned the note to the envelope which contained her return address and wrote a missive of his own. Someone would have to read it to her, and he felt distressed that a stranger should be privy to his most intimate thoughts. He rubbed his temples with his left hand elbow resting on the table. He had no need now to remain in town. When he'd finished, he sealed the letter in an envelope, crossed the street to the Stapleton's store, and posted it.

"You have a letter waiting for you," Mrs. Stapleton told him and went to fetch it.

Jeremy knew immediately from the envelope it was from Ireland, and he recognized his brother's slanted penmanship. He tore it open and perused the contents. His father had suffered a stroke that had left him paralyzed on the left side. A week later, a second stroke had ended his life. The landlord had then evicted his mother and brother. They were crowded into a neighbor's hovel made from bog peat. Shawn wrote that they had enough money for one passage to America. Could Jeremy send them enough for a second ticket?

How could a day that had started so auspiciously have ended so badly?

"Going back to the island?" Mrs. Stapleton asked.

"Yes," he replied, giving no further information as he turned to leave. He supposed he'd left the woman wondering if he'd been jilted.

Early the next morning, Jeremy got up and cooked breakfast by lantern light. He packed the few perishables that were left in the house, cleaned the kitchen, and left a brief note explaining to Jack and Agatha his intended return to the lighthouse. He informed them he would leave his extra key to Marion's house with Mrs. Stapleton. He knew they already had one key and would find his note left prominently on the table.

By nine thirty, he and Bailey sat in the dinghy headed toward the island. When they arrived, his temporary replacement, one Marcus Anderson, snored away in Jeremy's four-post bed. Jeremy would have let him sleep, but Bailey, excited by a stranger, barked so loudly the startled assistant keeper nearly fell out of bed.

"Bailey, hush," Jeremy commanded.

"You're back already?" Marcus sat up.

"Yeah, there's been a change of plans, but don't be in any hurry. We'll work together until you have to leave."

Marcus studied Jeremy's face and wisely decided to ask no questions.

"We'll take shifts at night and get more sleep."

"Won't your new wife come out?"

"No, not yet," Jeremy said. "Go on back to sleep."

\*\*\*\*

Abigail had never felt so weary. How could three children tire one so? Everett, of course, required the most attention. He had bolted and run off when they went outside after luncheon. But Ida Allen had assured her that a tall brick fence encircled the perimeter. Thankfully, Ida could see.

"I do worry about him tripping and falling. Still, he needs to expend some energy."

"I wish Bailey were here," Abbey said.

"Who's Bailey?"

"He's a wonderful dog, very gentle and protective. He'd follow after Everett and bring him back."

"Does he belong to your family?"

"He belongs to the man I'm going to marry," Abigail explained.

Now every bone in her body felt weary. She'd tried to teach Lucy some basic hand-sewing stitches to hem a garment and had pricked her fingers several times. Supper had been a tasteless meal of mashed potatoes and Boston beans, but mostly, her heart ached for Jeremy. What if he lost interest in her over the coming months? *Please Lord, don't let him forget me.*

The next day, Abigail made better progress with her sewing lessons. By the time she'd finished, Lucy had successfully secured four buttons to a vest and finished four button holes.

"These are very good," Abbey praised her. She had taught the child to center the sides of the vest, so that buttons and button holes lined up perfectly.

Lucy lifted Abbey's fingers to her lips and let her feel her smile.

Abbey hugged her, and Lucy hugged back with chubby arms. Next, she took some yarn and taught Lucy how to braid strands of matching lengths. "Once you've mastered this, I'll teach you to braid hair and tie ribbons," Abbey promised.

Abigail enjoyed her lively students, but her heart still ached for Jeremy. She longed for his gentle touch, the security of his strong arms, his melodic voice with its Irish brogue.

Christmas approached, and Abigail had never spent

a Christmas away from Arbor. With a pang that brought stinging tears to her eyes, she realized it would be her first Christmas without her father.

From the window, Ida Allen reported that light snow fell outside.

"Let's go outside!" Lucy said.

They all bundled up in coats, scarves, hats, and mittens to go to the courtyard.

"Stick out your tongues," Abbey encouraged them. "Taste the snow."

"It's so cold." Lucy giggled.

Abbey balled up a small snowball and held it up to Everett's cheek. He recoiled at first. She felt and heard him step back. But then curiosity overcame him. She removed his glove and spelled snow into his palm several times until he repeated the movements successfully in her own palm.

She wondered if it snowed at Lighthouse Island.

\*\*\*\*

"This winter storm is so dense, we should keep the light going during the day," Jeremy told Marcus.

The two men had established a growing comradery over the week they'd spent together. Jeremy had confided his situation with Abigail and his family's troubles back in Ireland.

"You know, Jeremy, I've been pondering your situation. I know for a fact there is going to be an opening for an assistant keeper at the Boston Light on Little Brewster Island. Boston would be a better place for your mother and brother. More jobs there than Maine. Besides isn't that where their ship will come in?"

"Yes," Jeremy replied. "Who is leaving Little

Brewster?"

"Michael Johnson is retiring. He says he's getting too old to climb all the stairs. If you're interested, I'd post a letter right away."

"Are you interested?"

"Well, I was. But if there's to be an opening here, I'd be just as willing." He grinned.

"Then I'd be near Abbey, and if she wanted to keep teaching, she could. I guess it couldn't hurt to apply."

"Nothing ventured, nothing gained, my mother always said," Marcus replied.

\*\*\*\*

Abigail finally received a letter handed to her by Matron. She hurried to her classroom and gave it to Ida.

"Who is it from? My aunt and uncle?"

"No, your lighthouse keeper," Ida replied with evident enthusiasm.

"What does it say? Oh, read it to me please!"

*My dearest Abbey,*

*I won't pretend I was not terribly disappointed by your decision, but I know you love your aunt and uncle. I just hope you still love me for you've become the light that warms my heart and gives me hope. If I can find a way to visit, I will. I've never been good with words, but I love you now and always.*

*Jeremy*

"How lovely and romantic," Ida said. "I wish I had a beau."

The children had gone to lunch, and the two young women were alone in the empty classroom. Abigail swiped unbidden tears from her eyes with the back of her hand.

"We would have been married by now and soon

celebrating our first Christmas together if my aunt hadn't interfered." She sniffed.

"Maybe he'll come to see you!" Ida said. "You must be ready with your Christmas present for him."

"I've been knitting him a scarf."

"Then finish it and mail it as soon as possible, so he'll get it in time."

"That's just what I'll do." Abigail's spirits lifted. She squeezed her new friend's hands.

"We should get gifts for our students too," Ida said. "I'm sure no one will remember Everett. His parents have five other children. They rarely visit."

As usual, thinking of others helped Abbey think less about her own problems. She would make Lucy a rag doll with braided yarn pigtails. She would make Jimmy and Everett small wooden boats that could float on the water. Of course, her carving skills were not as honed as Jeremy's, but she could manage some miniature canoes from thick downed branches in the schoolyard.

Chapter Eleven

"When God closes a door, he always opens a window" was an expression Jeremy had often heard his mother use. Perhaps God was pointing him in a new direction even now. As Marcus had suggested, he sat at the kitchen table and wrote a letter to the Light Keeping Service Headquarters in Boston. If he posted it tomorrow, it should arrive before Christmas Day. How he wished he could visit Abbey for the holidays, but the passage for his brother had taken most of his savings, and he'd not receive his salary again until after Christmas.

Suddenly, he heard Marcus crashing down the stairs and Bailey barking wildly.

"There's a ship caught on the shoal offshore. The waves are battering her, and she's breaking apart!"

Jeremy raced Marcus back up the stairs and used a telescope to locate the vessel, the *Armond*. The stranded ship resembled a beached whale, listing to starboard and surrounded by the violently churning ocean. Rain poured down in gray ribbons.

"Anyone in water as cold as 'tis will quickly die of hypothermia," he warned Marcus. "We'll use the Manby Mortar ta send a line out."

"The what?" Marcus asked.

"Oh, what do you call them here? A Lyle gun."

"Yeah. We trained with them."

"Hurry, we've no time to lose."

They quickly descended the stairs and retrieved the equipment from the shed.

"Pray the wind doesn't throw the line off course," Jeremy said as they pulled the cannon-like device to the rocky shore and aimed it at the ship's location. He lit the fuse, and a deafening explosion and kickback propelled the hawser across the sea toward its target.

Muffled by the wind, cheers from the crew erupted.

"They'll secure the rope around the mast and send the lead head and line back to us. We'll attach the breeches buoy on a block and tackle and get it to them."

"We'll only be able to evacuate one man at a time. We won't be able to save them all before the ship breaks apart on the rocks," Marcus said.

"Can you work the ropes here?" Jeremy asked.

"Yes."

"Then I'm taking a boat out."

Jeremy raced to the shed and donned a cork life vest before shoving the dinghy out into the waves and hopping aboard. Bailey whined at having been left behind and paced at the water's edge barking. They heard the boom of the ship's cannon returning the line.

It took tremendous pull on the oars to maneuver the boat out past the waves to the floundering ship. The icy wind made Jeremy's nose numb and his cheeks raw. The crash and roar of the waves deafened him. When he finally reached the *Armond*, the captain put a rope ladder over the starboard side and sent five men down one by one.

Jeremy helped them aboard, trying to maintain balance in the rocky boat.

"I'll spell you on the oars," volunteered one of the

sailors.

Jeremy let the man take his place. Overhead, a passenger in the breeches buoy slid toward the island. The buoy looked like a round flotation device with a pant-like harness into which the person's legs were inserted.

As soon as the five men were unloaded ashore, Jeremy rowed back to the ship.

"Can you take six this time?" the coxswain called down.

"Yes, I'll try," Jeremy said, hoping the boat would not swamp in the waves.

Again another sailor took the oars as Jeremy manned the rudder.

"How many aboard?" he shouted up to the captain.

"Twenty more."

"I'll be back!"

Another crew member dangled over the raging surf in the buoy. Sleet began to sting Jeremy's face and exposed hands. His panting breath escaped in moist clouds. The sailor strained against the oars. Once ashore, the men staggered through the shallow surf and collapsed.

For a third round, Jeremy headed back. This time Bailey jumped into the boat and refused to get out.

"Ya stubborn dog," Jeremy scolded.

They picked up five more sailors, but as they rowed toward shore, a huge breaker overturned the boat. Everyone including the oarsman tumbled out into the bucking sea.

Jeremy had never been so cold in his entire life. His teeth chattered in his head. He floundered to stay afloat. And then he slipped under. Everything went black.

****

As a gift to the matron, Abigail had secretly been teaching her students as well as others to sing the Christmas carols she played on the piano in the multipurpose room. Their hodgepodge of innocent voices ranged from lilting soprano to mellow tenor. None of the boys had reached adolescence, so their voices had not yet changed. The children learned "Away in a Manger," "Silent Night," and "O Come All Ye Faithful." Only Everett was unable to participate. Abigail ached for the child.

Matron Bards had told Abbey, Ida, and the other teachers that each child would receive an orange, some hard stick penny candy, and a Braille book for Christmas.

"The Boston Society for the Blind raised the money for the books. We will keep them in the library, and all the children can enjoy reading each other's gifts."

Abigail had finished knitting Jeremy's scarf and mailed it to Arbor with a carefully written note enclosed: "May this scarf and my love keep you warm. Merry Christmas."

She'd hoped to receive another letter from him and tried to hide her despondency when none arrived. Then a package came.

Ida read the enclosed note.

*Dear Abigail,*

*Your uncle and I had hoped to come for Christmas, but we had a real blizzard here, and Uncle Jack has been down with a fever. I hope you are settling into the routine there, and I know you are an excellent teacher.*

*Hope this gift will make the holiday brighter.*

*Love,*

*Aunt Agatha*

Abigail opened the package.

"Oh, Abbey, it's a beautiful shawl. Emerald green with lovely fringe," Ida enthused.

Abbey fingered the soft yarn, very fine and luxurious. It would keep her warm, but not as warm as Jeremy would have kept her.

Why had she heard nothing from him on Christmas Eve?

\*\*\*\*

The crew from the *Armond* had righted the rescue boat and located the oars bobbing on the churning surf. They shivered inside the bucking dinghy. Their teeth chattered so hard they thought they'd break. Then across the swells, they saw the black Lab dog-paddling for all he was worth. A man's arm dangled from his mouth, the body floated inertly on the water.

"Heave him on board!" shouted a sailor. "It's the light keeper."

Arms reached out across the wild surf.

"Don't swamp the boat!"

They dragged Jeremy's body over the side and dumped in the bottom of the dinghy. He could see himself in the bottom of the boat as though he hovered in the air above. He no longer felt the cold. A warm light broke through the storm clouds above beckoning him.

"I think he's dead," one of the sailors said.

"Pump his chest, and let's get to shore," said another.

"What about the dog?"

"He's halfway to shore already."

\*\*\*\*

Abigail tried to be happy for the children who had pulled down the socks they'd hung in the multipurpose room and spilled the contents on the floor. She heard some oohing over their books.

"I got *A Christmas Carol!*"

"I got *Little Women.*"

Others, from the sticky feel of their fingers, had already started to lick their candy. Abbey held a fragrant orange to Everett's nose and let him smell its deliciousness. Then she helped him peel it and separated the juicy fruit into sections he could pop into his mouth. But she had to swallow back her own disappointment.

Christmas dinner, prepared and delivered by some ladies from the Congregational Church, included turkey and yams, green beans, ambrosia, and yeasty rolls with melting butter as well as cakes and pies. Afterward, Abbey played the piano again and taught them "Joy to the World." But there was little joy in her own heart as she wondered why Jeremy had completely forgotten her.

She waited until dusk when she and Ida helped the boys take baths to give Jimmy and Everett their boats. They let them float in the soapy water and bob up and down. *Oh, Jeremy would have made them so much better with masts and sails.*

She gave Lucy her rag doll with its pink and white gingham dress and ruffled pinafore that she had made herself. The doll's yarn hair carefully formed two braids.

"Your doll can sleep with you at night."

"I like her pigtails," the little girl said. "I'm going to name her Abbey. Will you sleep with me too? Sometimes I get scared."

"Yes," Abigail said. "For just this one night, I'll sleep with you."

Lucy led her to the room she shared with three other girls. Abigail helped her change into a nightgown and then slipped into bed beside her. Lucy put her hands together and closed her eyes.

"And thank you, God, for sending Abigail to be our new teacher," the little girl said. She gave Abbey a soft kiss on the cheek and patted it gently. "You remind me of my mommy. She couldn't bring me home this Christmas because my little brother is sick, and she doesn't want me to catch it. But she will visit soon."

"I'm glad," Abbey said. "I know you miss her. It's hard to be away from someone you love."

Lucy nodded agreement.

Soon, by the soft, peaceful sound of Lucy's breathing, Abigail knew the child had drifted off into peaceful rest. Abigail wiped back the tears that dampened her own pillow, slipped out of the narrow bed, and up to her cold empty cot in the attic.

\*\*\*\*

"What do you think, doctor?" Marcus asked. "His fever has been high. I've only been able to get a small bit of broth into him."

Dr. Benson, a balding general practitioner with tufts of white hair above his ears, straightened up from bending over Jeremy's chest. His wrinkled forehead betrayed his anxiety over his patient. "He's got pneumonia. I can hear the fluid in his lungs. You're doing all you can."

Marcus had gone for the doctor the day after the storm as most of the crew recuperated at the lighthouse. They had lost four men and the captain. Now the assistant keeper helplessly paced Jeremy's room.

"If you're a praying man, pray for him," Benson advised as he shut his black bag. "We'll make a poultice of cooked onions to loosen the congestion in his chest, and I want you to give him a shot of whiskey twice a day to help him cough up the phlegm. We'll know something definite in a few days."

"I'm sorry to bring you out here on Christmas day," Marcus said.

"It couldn't be helped. He has a tremendous will to live."

"He's supposed to marry a girl he adores. She's all he talks about."

"What's with the dog?" the doctor asked, indicating Bailey who lay on the floor before the fireplace at the foot of Jeremy's bed. The lab looked up with woeful dark eyes.

"Bailey saved his life," Marcus explained.

"He's not looking too well himself. Better give him a shot of whiskey twice a day too." The doctor winked and grinned.

"I'd better write a letter to Jeremy's betrothed," Marcus said. "Will you post it for me after I take you back to shore? I've already alerted most of the Arbor fishermen that the crew here needs to be taken to town. They're going to come over and row them back to the mainland."

"I might as well examine the rest of them while I'm here," the doctor said. "That was a brave thing, you two young men did."

"Still, we didn't save everyone, and the captain went down with the ship."

Chapter Twelve

Abigail could not help herself any longer. She left the classroom the next day to have a good cry alone in her room.

Ida came to check on her. "Whatever is wrong?"

"I've heard nothing from Jeremy this Christmas. Either something awful has happened to him, or he no longer cares for me at all."

"Nothing could have happened in such short a time to change his mind." Ida comforted her.

"Ida, do you believe in prayer?"

"Yes, I do. I'm a Catholic, and I attend mass at St. James's."

"Could you take me there? I want to pray and speak to the priest."

"That would be Father William. I can take you there this afternoon during our free time."

"Thank you." Abbey squeezed her hand.

After the midday meal, Ida walked Abbey to St. James's and wisely left her friend to speak to the priest alone in his office.

"Please sit down, Miss Morrison." He politely helped her to a chair.

"I'm a bit nervous. I've never spoken to a priest before."

Father William gave a throaty chuckle. "I promise I don't bite."

Abigail spilled out her entire story, and he listened without interruption.

"My parents were Irish immigrants themselves," he said when she'd finished. "My father was a blacksmith from Tipperary. Your Jeremy sounds like a hard-working lad. But I do understand your aunt and uncle's concerns. Life is full of uncertainties, and an education and work experience are useful things."

"I know, but something is wrong. Something has happened to him. It's a feeling I have."

"I had that experience once myself. After finishing school at Montreal Sulpician College, I went to the Seminary of Saint Sulpice in Paris. One of my greatest mentors, Bishop Denis Affree, ordained me in 1845. I returned to Boston, but when the Second French Revolution was at its height, I grew very concerned about my former teacher. I prayed for him a great deal, but later learned that he'd been killed at one of the barricades during that horrible time. He was always a man who cared for the needs of the common people. Now, I'm not saying anything dire has happened to your Jeremy. Nor do I think he no longer cares for you. Write your aunt and uncle and find out."

"It takes so long to get letters back and forth," Abbey complained.

"Ah, the impatience of the young. Things will work themselves out in God's good time. If you'd like, I will pray with you."

Abbey obediently bowed her head and listened to the priest's comforting supplications to God on her behalf.

But back at the academy, she continued to worry. "When I did not return home with my aunt, Jeremy must have taken it as a betrayal. I must go home. I must return to Arbor, Ida. Help me please."

"What do you want me to do?" Ida asked, leery of getting into trouble.

"I want you to take my money and buy me a train ticket home."

"But, Abbey, you promised your aunt."

"I promised to try, but I don't belong here."

"The children love you. Lucy especially has taken such a liking to you. She'll be distraught if you leave. You're a talented teacher."

"I have to find out what has happened to Jeremy. If he no longer cares for me, I will return."

"But, Abbey, a blind woman traveling alone? Anything could happen."

"I'll stay in my seat and not get off until the depot in Portland."

"And then what? You'll still need to get to Arbor."

"I'll find a ride at the livery stable. I have to tell him in person why I made the decision that I did. I don't even know if my aunt gave him the letter I wrote."

\*\*\*\*

Marcus took Jeremy a bowl of hot broth and helped him to sit up against the pillows.

"I know, I know, I've got ta eat," Jeremy said. "It's ya mantra." He coughed, and his lungs rattled. But he managed to drink down the entire bowl. "Ta tell ya the truth, I think the whiskey does more for me."

Marcus laughed. "That's to follow. Thought you might want to look at these first. It was brought out by one of the boatmen picking up the crew of the *Armond*." He handed Jeremy a wrapped box and a letter.

Seeing the return address, Jeremy grabbed the box first and tore it open. His hands ran lovingly over the soft, warm wool scarf. Eagerly he read her note. "Blimey, I've missed Christmas, haven't I? What day is it?"

"December 27."

"What? She'll think I didna care enough ta send a present or a letter." He started to swing his legs out of bed but was stopped by a coughing fit.

"Whoa! You're not going anywhere."

"Then bring me paper! Bring me ink!" he shouted between raspy exhalations.

"Open the other letter."

"What? Oh, yes." He opened the envelope and perused the contents written on official Light Keeping Service stationery. "I can have the assistant position on Little Brewster Island!" he said. "I can be there when me mam and brother arrive in America."

"Then you've got to rest and get your strength back. I think this calls for two whiskeys. One for you and one for me."

Bailey barked letting them know he'd take a third.

"I'm well enough ta travel," Jeremy insisted. "My fever is gone and except for this residual cough, I'm better."

"I'd feel better if it was the doctor saying it instead of you," Marcus said, his freckled brow lined with concern.

"Abbey must wonder what's happened ta me. I want ta let her know in person that I didn't forget her at Christmas, that she's never far from my thoughts."

"I'll row you to the mainland, and we'll rent a

wagon from the livery to get to Portland. After you take the train, I'll return the wagon. Have you got money for the return train ticket?"

"Yes," Jeremy said, coughing a little.

"Today is December 27$^{th}$. We'll leave first thing tomorrow morning. Bailey and I will keep the light burning while you're gone." Marcus combed his fingers back through his red hair.

"This has been more than you bargained for," Jeremy said.

"I've learned a lot, and you've been a great mentor. Just hope I can deal with the solitude once you move on to Little Brewster. It's pretty lonesome out here."

"You need a dog. A good swimmer like Bailey."

"I was thinking more in terms of a wife. Does Abigail have a sister?"

Jeremy laughed but soon returned to coughing. "I'll ask if she has a friend."

****

As Ida and Abbey had planned, the young women left Pearson Academy at five o'clock on Thursday morning, December 28$^{th}$, and met Abbey's prearranged hansom at the corner. Everyone else at the academy still slumbered in their beds.

Ida embraced Abbey with tears slipping down her cheeks. "I'm going to miss you! Write me as soon as you get there, so I'll know you're safe. Please come back and visit."

"I will," Abbey promised. "I feel bad about not saying good-bye to the children, but they might have leaked the news to Matron Bard."

"I'll try to soften the blow. I don't know how I'll handle Everett without you."

"Just keep spelling words into his hand. They're beginning to make sense."

"But he'll want you and will probably pitch a royal fit." She grasped Abbey gently by the upper arms. "Whatever happens, Abbey, remember we really need you here."

Ida helped her friend into the hansom cab along with her meager belongings and then paid the driver. Abbey sank back against the cushioned seat. The frosty air had chilled her to the bone, but inwardly the prospect of being with Jeremy again warmed and excited her. They bumped over the cobblestone streets of Boston until they reached the train depot, where the driver helped her out of the carriage and walked her to the ticket window.

"Train to Portland on time?" he asked.

"Yes, it is. Due in the station at six."

"Got any room where this young lady could sit inside? It's awful cold out here."

"Sure. Come on in. I've a small stove with a pot of coffee."

Inside, the ticket office felt cramped but blessedly warm. Abbey even unwrapped her scarf and set it in her lap, while she let her fingers heat up around the hot cup of coffee. Even the inviting smell of it was reassuring.

"Bad day to be traveling," the ticket vender said. "Hope you chose an enclosed car."

"I did," Abbey said.

"Could be more snowfall, and you're heading farther north?"

"I'm used to it," she said. "I've lived in Maine all my life until recently."

"Well, lots of folks headed back up to New

Hampshire and such now that Christmas is over."

Abbey heard him ruffle open a newspaper. "Been a shipwreck off the coast of Arbor. Ever heard of Arbor?"

"Yes," Abbey said. "That's where I grew up. What does the article say?"

"On December 15, the *Armond,* an American cargo vessel, was caught on a shoal off Arbor, Maine, and battered in gale force winds that ripped it apart. The Light Keeping Service rescued most of the crew. The captain, George Willows of Nantucket, and four crewman drowned. The crewmen were Samuel Stone of Salem, Massachusetts; George Bentley of Portland, Maine; Josiah Pickett of Newport, Rhode Island; and William Mills of Bridgetown, Massachusetts. All cargo was lost at sea. The ship was insured by Lloyds of London."

"Rescued by the light keepers? I've been to Lighthouse Island. I know the keeper. Does it say if he is safe?"

"No mention of his name, but I feel sure the reporter would have included him in the list of dead, if he hadn't made it."

Abigail swallowed a knot of fear that welled in her throat. "Yes, I'm sure you're right."

She drank the coffee and waited for the train. When it finally arrived, the ticket vender called a conductor over to help her aboard. She settled back in her seat.

*Only a few hours and I'll be in his arms again.*

She tingled with longing and excitement.

Chapter Thirteen

At the Arbor livery stable, Marcus paid Roger Simms for the use of a wagon and two horses, promising to return both by midafternoon.

"You'll be responsible for any damages done to the wheels or harness," Simms warned. "Avoid ruts. And make sure the horses get water. I keep a pail in the back of the wagon."

As Simms went about his business hitching the team, Jeremy excused himself.

"I'll collect our pay from the post office, then look around the store a bit. I'll be back in a moment," Jeremy said. He crossed to the mercantile and perused the merchandise, looking for a belated Christmas present for Abbey. Finally, he found a cameo brooch. She'd be able to touch the raised profile with her sensitive fingertips.

"Do you have a box for it?" he asked Mrs. Stapleton.

"Yes," she said, reaching under the counter. "I could wrap it for you if you like."

"Thank you."

After crossing the street, he climbed up on the leather seat next to Marcus.

"Oh no, you don't. You're going to lie down in the back with this blanket completely pulled up."

"It's not necessary," Jeremy complained.

"In the back, or we're not going."

Grumbling, Jeremy obeyed.

\*\*\*\*

In Portland, Abbey debarked, bumping along with the crowd of passengers. She carried her purse and a carpetbag full of clothes. She used her cane to maneuver the platform, tapping it back and forth in front of her.

"May I 'elp you, miss?" a pleasant, masculine voice asked.

"Could you direct me to the ticket counter?"

"Of course." Abbey felt for an extended arm and took it. They walked forward.

"Mind the step up," the man said.

She obeyed, touching the stair first with the toe of her shoe.

"'Ere we are."

She let go of his arm.

"Yes, can I be of service?" another male voice asked.

"I need a dependable ride from here to Arbor," she said.

"To Arbor, you say. I dunno of anyone going in that direction, miss."

"I could take you to Arbor," said the first voice. "My name is Michael Gregory, and I have an old rig and team nearby."

"What do I owe you for the trip?" Abbey asked.

"I don't want your money, miss. I'm 'eaded in that direction anyway. 'Ere let me take your bag."

Abbey was a bit skeptical. With hesitation, she handed him the carpetbag and held onto his arm as they departed the depot and crossed the busy street. The swoosh of a passing carriage caused her skirt to billow, and she grabbed hold of her hat to keep it from blowing off.

"Thank you for helping me navigate, Mr. Gregory."

"I'll put your bag in the back. You just step up 'ere."

Abbey pulled herself up into the buggy and adjusted her skirt.

Gregory joined her on the left side the seat and turned the animals in the right direction. Then he called out, "Haw!"

The conveyance lurched forward, and Abbey grabbed the arm rail. She gripped tightly as they bumped along. Soon the sounds of the town faded, and Abbey felt awkward. She wondered what to say to Mr. Gregory. But he spoke first.

"You 'aven't told me your name."

"Abigail."

"And why are you going to Arbor?"

Did she detect a less friendly tone? "I live there, and my aunt and uncle live there."

"They're expecting you?"

"Yes," she lied.

"Why didn't they come to pick you up?"

"I didn't want them to come because they're elderly."

They rode on in silence for what Abigail judged to be an hour, though she couldn't be sure.

"That's an interesting ring you're wearing around your neck," Gregory said. "Real gold?"

She felt him finger the ring on the chain which lay against her breast. Suddenly, he jerked the reins back and then snapped the chain from around her neck. Abbey's heart pounded as he grabbed her and pressed his lips against hers. His grizzly chin abraded her soft skin. His breath smelled of stale cigars.

"Don't!" she screamed, shoving him away with both hands flat against his chest. She jumped from the carriage, then slapped the horse or mule on the rump and shouted,

"Haw!"

The wagon bolted forward, but she did not know if Gregory was still on it. She raced in the opposite direction back toward Portland literally running blind. Her mind jumped from one thought to another.

*Is he turning around? Am I too visible on the road?*

She bolted off the snow-crusted dirt road and scrambled up the steep embankment. *Do I hear the wheels of the carriage returning?* Darting into the woods, she banged into a tree and staggered backward. She'd injured her forehead and wrenched her neck.

*Think! Think! What can I use as a weapon?*

She dropped to the ground and felt snow five to six inches deep.

*I've left an obvious trail, easy to follow.*

*Don't panic! God help me!*

Groping around, she found a sturdy branch to wield as a club. As she crawled forward, her dress caught on reeds and stubble. Then she touched ice, slick and cold, part of some pond. There she wouldn't leave a trail, but she would be more visible. Could the ice hold her weight? She slid forward easing herself across the surface, then veered right, hugging the rim until she felt some large boulders. She crawled behind them and balled up for warmth, gathering her skirt tight around her body, hoping to make herself invisible. She pulled up the hood of her long woolen cape and waited.

As she sat there shivering, she realized Gregory, if that was his real name, had her purse, her bag containing Jeremy's love spoon, and her money. Tears streamed down her face.

*At least, my wedding gown wasn't in the carpetbag.* She tried to comfort herself.

Hours passed, and the temperature dropped. Even her teeth chattered. Weary and thirsty, she was still afraid to come out of hiding. She took snow from the ground and let it melt in her mouth. She had no idea of the time.

Taking off her knee-length cape, she curled upon the damp ground and put the woolen drape completely over herself making a wool igloo with only a tiny space to breathe. Gradually, her shivering subsided. The trapped body heat gave warmth, and she dozed fitfully.

When Abbey awoke stiff and achy, she had no idea how long she'd slept or whether it was night or day. Her head throbbed, and she gingerly felt the bruised knot on her forehead. She reached out and grabbed a handful of snow to put over it, but the cold only made it hurt more.

She lay still and listened acutely. After a while she heard an owl hoot, and later a wolf howled somewhere in the distance.

*Wolves! What should I do if a pack arrives?* She groped around and found her make-shift club. *Please God, help me!*

She hoped she blended in with the rocks and snow. Her fingers, nose, and toes were numb. She rubbed and moved and massaged them, waiting for morning. After a while, she heard the cheerful song of birds heralding dawn. Abbey gathered the courage to leave her shelter and relieve herself in the woods. Her stomach growled. She ate some more snow.

****

True to his word, Marcus had gotten Jeremy to the Portland train station. At the depot, they'd parted company. Jeremy had purchased his ticket and slept most of the way as the train traveled on through New Hampshire to Massachusetts.

Now he stood before the Pearson Academy for the Blind, an imposing brick building with Corinthian columns. He felt a surge of joy and anticipation at seeing Abbey again. Inside, he introduced himself to Matron Bards.

"I'm here to see Abigail Morrison."

"Abigail? But Abigail has returned to Arbor."

"What? When?" His voice was dismayed.

"She left early yesterday morning. But it was not with my permission."

"She traveled alone?"

"Let me fetch Ida Allen for you. She can explain it with greater detail."

As Bards disappeared, Jeremy sank into a chair.

*If she left yesterday, she should have been in Arbor this morning. Surely Mrs. Stapleton would have known, but she'd have said something this morning. I'm sure Marion's house was empty when we passed it this morning. Maybe she went to her aunt and uncle's farm. But what if she never made it to Arbor at all? Where is she?*

Matron Bards returned accompanied by a young woman with chestnut hair drawn back from her broad brow.

"Miss Allen was Abbey's co-teacher. Perhaps she can tell you more accurately what happened." Matron Bards' lips formed a thin line, stern and judgmental.

"Mr. McKetcheon, Abbey has told me so much about you." Ida extended her hand. "She was worried when she didn't hear from you at Christmas and said she had to go home. I bought the ticket for her, and she took a hansom to the Boston depot at Causeway and Andover Streets early yesterday."

"But how can that be? I don't think she ever reached Arbor."

Fear fell over Ida's face. She swallowed deeply. "You must find her. I'll never be able to live with myself if something has happened to her."

\*\*\*\*

Jeremy quickly retraced his route to the Boston depot.

"Yes." The man at the ticket counter of the B & L line assured him a blind woman had taken the 7:30 train to Portland on December 27th.

"I want a one-way ticket to Portland now," Jeremy said. "When does the next train leave?"

"1:10."

"That long?" Jeremy groaned but gave the man the money.

Time crept by as he waited, often looking up at the depot clock in exasperation. When he could sit no longer, he paced back and forth like a pendulum. Soft flakes fell on his head and shoulders. He brushed them from his black wool coat. When the train finally arrived, loud and steaming, he waited impatiently for the passengers to disembark, then took the steps two at a time to enter the passenger carriage. He took a seat by the window and brooded.

*Faster, faster* Jeremy seemed to hear in the *click-clack* of the iron wheels over the rails. Taking the same earlier route in reverse, he stared out the window as they chugged along at sixty miles per hour. Though it was much faster than any horse, it didn't seem fast enough.

He was the first person out of his seat waiting at the door when they pulled into Portland. He darted through the crowd straight to the ticket office, where he shoved to the front of the line. "Please, I need to speak ta someone right away."

"Wait your turn!" an angry traveler behind him snapped.

"This is very important. I don't need a ticket. I need information. Did you work here yesterday?" he asked the man behind the ticket counter.

"Yep, work here most days."

"Do you remember a blind girl getting off a train from Boston?"

"Yes, I do. She walked with a cane."

"How did she leave the station?"

"She was with a fella she seemed to know. He offered her a ride in his carriage."

"Who was he?"

"I don't know. You're holding up the line."

"She never arrived in Arbor."

"I'm sorry, but I never saw the fella before."

"Thank you."

Jeremy looked at the people glaring behind him.

*Don't panic. Maybe the carriage broke down, a wheel busted by a rut in the road.*

*Maybe they took shelter with a farmer from the snow storm. Maybe she is at her aunt and uncle's house. But maybe she's been abducted or worse. God, I wish I'd brought Bailey.*

He crossed the busy street where he'd seen a livery stable and quickly explained Abbey's disappearance.

"I saw a man leave with a woman Tuesday. I'd never seen either of them before. That's why I remember," said Jacob Hankins, the owner. "You're going to need help if you're going to find her, and it'll be dark soon."

Jeremy sighed with frustration, knowing that the man was right. "Look, I'm out of money, and I feel like I'm running out of time."

"You bed down with me and my two sons tonight. We have lodgings behind the stable. They'll start out with you in the morning at first light, and I'll provide the horses."

\*\*\*\*

Abbey could tell the day was dying, the sunlight ebbing. The air had grown chillier. Her fingers, nose, and toes were numb. She rubbed and moved and massaged them. How she dreaded another night among the boulders. Her stomach was so empty that it churned endlessly and cramped painfully.

She shook snow off her cape and curled up under it again. After a while, she slept.

She awoke to the howling of wolves. This time they were much closer. Her fingers wrapped around the club.

She heard growling and imagined their fierce teeth. She'd heard stories of wolves surrounding a big bull moose and bringing it down, tearing open its neck. The silver timber wolves were large brutes with little fear of humans. Abigail tensed remaining perfectly still as she heard and smelled their approach. A branch snapped. She jumped involuntarily.

*I can't spend another night here.*

A low growl erupted outside her cape. The muffled sound of front paws digging in the snow terrified her. She felt a canine body bump against hers with nothing separating her but a thick wool material.

****

After a sleepless night, Jeremy sat astride a bay mare in a creaking saddle, clomping down the road from Portland to Arbor, sick with growing despair. Whatever tracks might have been left by horses and wagon wheels were obliterated by snow.

"Abbey! Abbey!" he shouted every few minutes, his voice growing increasingly hoarse.

Then Davy Hankins took up the call. His chestnut gelding pricked its ears. Both Davy and his brother Chandler carried loaded rifles. Both were experienced hunters and trackers. After a while, Davy reined in his horse and pointed at the gray sky above the forest where turkey buzzards flew in a circle.

Jeremy understood the significance.

"Chandler, stay with the horses," Davy said. "I'll investigate."

"I'm coming with you," Jeremy said as he dismounted. He gave the reins of the mare to Chandler and followed Davy up the embankment beside the road. His heart pounded when they found crimson blood stains over the pure white snow. Wolf tracks were imprinted in the drifts, and a trail where a carcass had been dragged led into a thicket. A hideous-looking buzzard perched on an icy bush.

Jeremy rushed forward. He found the carrion-eater tearing flesh from the carcass of a doe. The stench of death hung in the airs. The gruesome raptors resembled demons.

Jeremy expelled his breath in relief. "Abigail!" he shouted.

The booming of his voice did not scatter the vultures.

\*\*\*\*

Huddled beneath her cape, Abigail thought she heard the muffled sound of her name. *It's just the wind howling.*

But then it came again. "Abigail!"

She threw off the cape and stood, but her head spun. Her forehead throbbed. For a moment, she swayed ready to faint. "I'm here!" she shouted. "I'm here?"

"Abigail!"

She turned in the direction of the sound and stumbled forward. She must remember the pond. Stooping down, she crawled toward the ice trying to retrace the route to the road.

"I'm here!" she shouted again. She walked with her arms outstretched to avoid the trees. She reached the embankment and half fell, half rolled down toward the road. She stood on trembling legs with tears streaming down her face.

"I'm here," she said weakly.

She heard footsteps crunching through the snow and thin, low lying branches snapping. Then strong arms pulled her up, enveloped her in warmth.

"Abbey, it's me." Jeremy's voice calm and

reassuring. His finger gingerly touched the bruised area of her swollen, throbbing forehead. "What happened?"

"Jeremy, I lost everything—my purse, my clothes, and your love spoon. He even took the wedding band I purchased for you from the goldsmith in Boston. I thought he was nice, but he was a brute."

"What did he do ta you?"

"Grabbed me, but I jumped off the wagon and ran. I was afraid he'd find me. I've been hiding in the woods for two nights."

"It's a wonder you didn't freeze ta death. You've had nothing ta eat? What about your forehead? It looks like someone beat you."

"I ran into a tree trying to get away."

"We'll get you back to Portland." He pulled the hood up on her cape and led her back through the forest to the road. Then Jeremy helped her get her foot in the stirrup of his saddle. He boosted her up and swung up behind her. Davy and Chandler, mounted as well, turned their horses toward Portland.

Chapter Fourteen

At Jacob Hankins's home, Davy heated split pea soup, ladled it up in bowls, and passed them around the table. Chandler cut some slices of hard crusted bread, and Jacob sat back with his steaming cup of coffee.

"That's quite an adventure you've been through," he told Abbey. "Smart enough to completely cover yourself from the elements with that cape."

"I was worried about the wolves," Jeremy said.

"I can see why you were so worried," Hankins said. "Abbey's a fine little slip of a woman. I've got some tobacco you can put over that bruise. Help it heal right up."

Jeremy coughed, putting the back of his hand across his mouth to stop the spread of germs.

"You don't sound well," Abbey said.

"It's nothing. You eat. You look exhausted."

Abbey tasted the soup. "It's really good," she said. "I ate snow. It calmed my thirst but not my appetite."

"I sure would like ta get my hands on tha man who robbed ya," Jeremy said. "What did he say his name was?"

"Michael Gregory. But I don't think it was his real name."

"Never heard of anyone around here by that name," Davy said.

"Probably some rover or con artist," Chandler said.

"I just hope I never encounter him again." Abbey shivered.

Later, when the Hankinses had all gone back to work, Jeremy sat down with Abbey to explain about the shipwreck and his recovery.

"You shouldn't be out of bed!" she reprimanded.

"I'm fine," he insisted. "And I have some news. My father passed away."

"Jeremy, I'm so sorry." Abbey hugged him.

"He had a long life but a hard one. I hope his soul is at peace."

"Surely it is."

"My mother and brother are coming ta Boston from Wexford."

"When?"

"In March. I've arranged a transfer ta the light on Little Brewster Island."

"You did it for me, didn't you?"

He nodded and smoothed her hair back from her forehead. "If ya like working at the school, ya can still work, but ya don't have ta."

"I don't want us to be separated ever again." She kissed his cheek.

\*\*\*\*

The next morning, Davy volunteered to take them back to Arbor and dropped them off at the Thompson farm.

"I can't thank you enough for finding her," Agatha told Jeremy.

"You've only yourself to blame for thinking you can manage other people's lives," Uncle Jack warned.

"Our situation has changed," Abbey said. "You were right, Aunt Agatha, I did like working at the academy, and I want to return, but I had to know about Jeremy. I had to know why I hadn't heard from him at Christmas. That's why I had to come back."

"I've requested and been given a transfer ta the assistant keeper's position at Little Brewster in Boston Harbor. My mother and brother, Shawn, will be arriving in Boston in March. Abbey and I still want ta marry, but we're going ta wait till my family arrives. That is, if you'll grant your permission this time."

"I'm going to write a letter to Matron Bards explaining everything. I hope she'll take me back, but if not, perhaps she'll let me volunteer. I really loved the children."

"It seems we've grossly underestimated both of you, your strong commitment to one another, and your maturity." Uncle Jack looked at Agatha pointedly.

"And Aunt Agatha, I know this is going to be a huge adjustment for you, but I've decided to convert to Catholicism."

"I see," Agatha said resignedly.

"My friend and co-teacher at Pearson's is also Catholic, and I can worship Christ just as well in that faith. I've prayed about this decision a long time."

"Then it looks as if everything is settled," said Uncle Jack.

"There is one other matter I'd like ya ta consider. My brother is an experienced farmer and could easily learn ta be a lobsterman. If he can't find work in Boston, and Abbey and I pay a small rent for them, could he and my mother possibly come live in Marion's house?"

"The house is Abbey's as soon as she turns eighteen, and as long as the loan is paid, it will not be foreclosed. We'll try to contribute to the mortgage as well."

****

"Abigail, this is Marcus. He'll be staying on here permanently."

"So you're the person I owe the thanks for nursing Jeremy back from pneumonia," Abbey said, extending her hand. "How did you ever get this stubborn man to stay in bed?"

"It wasn't easy, believe me."

Bailey recognized Abbey's voice and bounded in gamboling round her as if greeting a long lost relative.

"Calm down, boy," Jeremy reprimanded. "We're not going ta let her out of our sights again."

"We've come ta pack up," he told Marcus. "I'm ta report ta Little Brewster next week."

"So do I hear wedding bells?"

"After my mother and brother arrive in Boston."

"You're officially invited if the Light Keeping Service can spare you. The ceremony will be at St. James's Cathedral. We'll let you know the date," Abbey said.

Jeremy crossed to the bedroom and pulled out an old seaman's trunk from beneath the bed. He began to fold and pack clothes as Abigail carefully wrapped his carvings in newspaper and stored them inside the chest.

"I'll be up cleaning the lantern and trimming the wicks," Marcus said, leaving them alone.

"My God, I've missed you," Jeremy said. "I'm so sorry about Christmas."

He pulled Abbey into his arms, and her heartbeat quickened. She anticipated and soon felt the soft pressure of his supple lips. She breathed in the masculine scent of him. Eagerly, she returned his kisses tingling with warmth that spread throughout her body. Jeremy's strong but gentle fingers caressed her shoulders and then moved to her waist. A soft sigh escaped her lips.

"I can't wait until you're my wife," Jeremy said in a husky voice.

Like a jealous chaperone, Bailey bounded into the room, stood on his hind legs, and joined them in a group hug. They both broke out laughing.

"I do have a Christmas present for you. I've been waiting for the right time ta give it ta you." He took the small wrapped box from his back pocket.

Abbey unwrapped it and felt the cameo. "It's lovely," she said. "Will you pin it to my collar?"

Jeremy drew near and attached the brooch to her gown. Abbey stood on tiptoe and kissed him again.

\*\*\*\*

At the Pearson Academy, Ida, Lucy, and the other students planned a welcome party for Abbey. The children cut strips of colored paper and glued rings of paper together to make a chain to decorate the room. They baked cookies and awaited her arrival.

"Will she be staying this time? I've missed her so much," Lucy said.

"She'll be with us during the week and go out to the lighthouse on Saturdays and Sundays."

"What's a lighthouse?" asked Molly, a new student with pigtails and a sprinkle of freckles across her tiny nose.

"It's a tower with a bright light at the top to help ships navigate the coast," Ida explained.

"How will she get to the lighthouse?"

"She'll take the ferry. It's a boat that transports passengers out to the islands around Boston and to Cape Cod."

"You're going to like Miss Morrison," Lucy told Molly. "She's very nice."

\*\*\*\*

This time, Jeremy and Abbey traveled together. Aunt Agatha and Uncle Jack had driven them to Portland after the letter from Matron Bards had arrived reinstating Abigail on the faculty.

The hardest part of the train trip was crating Bailey and putting him in a cargo car. He whimpered like a baby, and Abbey knew Jeremy's heart was breaking.

"It won't be long," she told the dog, kneeling down and letting him lick her fingers through the bars of his cage.

Inside the passenger car, she tried to distract Jeremy from fretting over Bailey. "I want you to meet Father William at St. James's. He has the kindest way about him," Abbey said as they sat side by side on the train.

"I will," Jeremy said. He held her small hand in his.

"Tell me more about your mother and brother," Abbey prompted.

"Well, my mother's name is Mary, and she grew up in Cork. Her father was a shepherd. I remember him a little. But her mother died before I was born. My mum likes ta sing and is an excellent seamstress. My brother Shawn is six years older than me. He has red hair like my mum.

"He was arrested once for being caught with the White Shirts, an Irish liberation group. We were afraid he'd be deported ta Australia, but my father and the local priest, Father Carmody, talked the magistrate into mercy and a second chance.

"My sister, Bridget, was a dark-haired, blue-eyed beauty but always thin and prone ta respiratory illnesses. She wanted ta come ta America and work in a grand house as a maid, but my parents wouldn't let her come ta a country where she had nary a relative nor friend. When I turned eighteen, they sent me ahead ta find a place for myself and for her when I'd established myself. But as ya know, she died before I could afford ta bring her over."

"Are you and Shawn close?"

"He was more like a second da, sort of bossy and demanding. But I do look forward ta seeing him again. And I've missed me mam."

"I hope she'll like me."

"Sure she will. Are you hungry? I can go ta the dining car and get a sandwich."

"That would be good." Abbey felt him get up and move up the aisle.

And then she heard it, the voice she would never forget—Michael Gregory's. She slid closer to the window hoping he'd not seen her. He had spoken to another passenger about an article in the newspaper, but she'd recognized his tone immediately.

Panicked, she didn't know whether to tell Jeremy or not. Was Gregory armed? If arrested, would anyone believe the testimony of an "eye" witness who couldn't see? But she wanted that wedding band back and Jeremy's love spoon.

*That crook has probably sold them by now.*

She shrank down in the seat trying to make herself

invisible. How many other unsuspecting people had this conman bamboozled or worse? She could have died in the snowy forest and freezing temperatures. Her face heated up with rage, and Jeremy returned to find her with an expression of inner agony upon her face.

"What are ya thinking of, luv?"

She jumped, suddenly startled.

"I'm sorry. I didn't mean ta surprise ya."

"Sit down," she said softly.

He handed her a roast beef sandwich with a slice of cheddar on a hard roll.

"Thank you," she murmured, still in a quandary.

As the train progressed through New Hampshire, Jeremy rested his head on Abbey's shoulder and slept. His warm breath tingled against her neck. She listened for Gregory's voice with focused concentration, but it too had grown silent.

When the train rumbled over the bridge spanning the Charles River, Jeremy awoke with a start and had to shake himself fully conscious and get his bearings.

"We're in Boston," he announced.

"We're in no rush," Abbey replied. "When we pull into the station, let's wait till the others disembark."

She hoped to remain inconspicuous and turned her head toward the window. Once the locomotive pulled into the station, the passengers moved from their seats. She heard the voice again coming up the aisle, impatient and cross at having to wait.

"What are you staring at outside the window?" Jeremy teased.

"Just letting the sun warm my face," Abbey said without turning to him.

Jeremy chuckled. "Well, come on. We're the last

passengers in the car."

She put on her hat and pulled it low. "Let me hold your arm," she said. "And you take my cane." She did not want to draw attention to herself as an unsighted person.

Jeremy tucked her hand in his and led her off the train.

\*\*\*\*

On the wooden platform, Gregory watched a couple leave the passenger car. He cupped his hand around a match and lit his cigar. Then inhaling the pungent smoke, he surveyed the crowded station in search of a possible dupe. Exhaling a foul cloud of odious fumes, his eyes roamed back to the couple. There was something familiar about the woman. He studied her as they went back to a cargo car, and a porter removed a cage containing a black Lab.

The man with the woman was muscular and somewhat formidable, but the right side of his face was badly scarred. The dog once removed from the cage looked formidable as well, though it demonstrated great affection for its owner.

Suddenly, it dawned on him. The girl—she was the blind woman he had picked up in Portland, the one who had escaped him. A moment of nervous tension passed.

*What does it matter? After all, she can never identify me.*

He shrugged his shoulders, threw down his cigar butt, and snuffed it with his scuffed boot.

\*\*\*\*

Jeremy and Bailey made sure that Abbey was safely back to the Pearson Academy, with her new travel trunk stored in her attic room.

"I'll get Ida to help me to the ferry on Friday," Abbey said. "You're sure the head keeper and his family won't consider me an inconvenience?"

"Mr. Rembold said his wife loves company. She gets island fever," Jeremy replied. "I'll miss ya till then." He drew her close and kissed her.

"I'll miss you too."

As Jeremy followed her down the stairs to the front entrance, he realized no one had reacted to his facial scars because none of the students could see. Bailey, however, had made numerous friends who petted him and tried to catch his lively, wagging tail.

Abbey's spirits deflated after Jeremy left, but she went to the classroom she shared with Ida.

"Abbey! You're back," Ida sang out.

Abigail could hear Lucy running to her and felt her embrace her skirts.

"I'm glad you're back," Lucy said. "Come feel the decorations we made for you."

She led Abbey to touch the chains.

"We have a new student," Ida added. "This is Molly. She's nine."

Abbey knelt and let Molly touch her face.

"I'm very glad to meet you," she told the child.

\*\*\*\*

Michael Gregory had followed the couple from the train station at a distance. He'd seen them enter the Pearson Academy for the Blind. *An entire school of possible victims,* he'd thought. He'd seen the man and the black Lab leave before he moved on to the less prosperous side of Boston near the docks. He worked on the wharves unloading cargo and sometimes pilfered small items to pawn. He'd saved enough since his immigration from London to purchase two mules and a wagon, which he also used to transport crates and possessions for new arrivals.

He'd always been careful to get rid of his ill-gotten trinkets at smaller towns around Boston even going as far as Portland. Adept at pickpocketing and the preparation of fraudulent documents for new immigrants, he'd been able to make his way in America.

Chapter Fifteen

Jeremy and Bailey road the ferry out to Little Brewster Island. The boat rose and fell with the waves, and the January air was biting but invigorating. The sun shone, and the azure blue sky lifted their spirits. Bailey's ears flapped back in the wind, and his long pink tongue lolled out of his mouth. He had anxiously sniffed every inch of the ferry and finally sank down at Jeremy's feet satisfied.

Jeremy watched the white tower of the Little Brewster lighthouse grow larger and larger. Sam Rembold, the head keeper, met them at the dock and moored the ferry, so they could disembark. He shook Jeremy's hand and led him up to the house, a two story with dormer windows.

"This is my wife, Carrie," Sam said, and Jeremy nodded to a petite woman with dark hair pulled back in a bun at the nape of her neck. She wore a plain gray dress covered by an apron and balanced a baby boy on her hip. Another boy with bright brown eyes clung to her skirts.

She smiled and dimples merrily dotted her cheeks. "Would you like cup of coffee or hot tea?" she offered.

"Coffee, thank you," he said and joined Sam in sitting at the table.

"I like your dog," said the boy who looked about five years of age.

"This is Sammy," Rembold said with pride.

"You can pet Bailey, Sammy. He likes ta be petted. Bailey has helped people who were drowning."

Carrie brought steaming mugs of coffee and set them on the table. "I'll let you men discuss procedures," she said. "Teddy needs a bath." She disappeared down the hall with the messy baby.

\*\*\*\*

Abbey was surprised by how easily she returned to the old routine. But at night when she lay alone in her narrow cot beneath the snow-covered eaves, she longed for Jeremy and counted the days left until Friday.

She heard her door creak open, and a small voice she recognized as Lucy's said, "Can you come see about Molly? She's crying. I think she's homesick."

"I know just the thing," Abbey told Lucy. Then getting out of bed, she padded barefooted across to her bags and removed several of Jeremy's wooden carvings.

They went back to the room that the girls shared, and Abbey let Molly feel the otter, the seagull, and the dog. Then she made up wonderful stories about them. Soon both girls were peacefully asleep.

Finally, Friday arrived, classes ended, and Ida walked Abbey to the ferry landing. When they walked near the loading docks, catcalls and whistles rang out from the leering stevedores and cargo workers. Ida increased their pace. At the landing, Abbey purchased her ferry ticket, then hugged her friend in parting.

"I dread walking past the docks again," Ida said. "I think I'll take a different route back."

"I don't blame you," Abbey replied.

\*\*\*\*

Knowing the time that the ferry was expected to moor at Little Brewster Island, Jeremy paced the dock with the collar of his wool jacket pulled up to protect his neck from the cold gale. He hoped Abbey had bundled up.

Then in the distance, he saw the ferry bucking over the waves. Abbey had her scarf pulled up over her mouth and nose for warmth. When she disembarked, he wrapped her in a bear hug. She kissed him enthusiastically not caring who saw them.

"My feet are frozen," she said as she drew back, stomping them on the dock.

"Let's get you in where it's warm."

Jeremy took her up to the main house and introduced her to Carrie and the boys. Mr. Rembold was upstairs sleeping after a long night of keeping watch.

"Let me show you your room," Carrie said, leading them both upstairs to a bedchamber with pastel blue walls, ruffled white curtains, and a narrow bed with a colorful patchwork quilt. Small but adequate, the room would be Abbey's retreat when she stayed on the island. Jeremy described it to her in detail.

Abbey stored her bags and then returned downstairs.

"I want to show ya the assistant's quarters," Jeremy said.

"Can I come too?" Sammy asked.

"Sammy, mind your manners," Carrie reprimanded.

"'Tis fine," Jeremy said. "Come on along."

"You're pretty," Sammy said to Abbey.

"Put on your jacket and mittens," his mother

warned.

He quickly obeyed and then trotted behind Abbey and Jeremy as they crossed the yard, passed the storage shed, and entered a cottage on the east side of the island. It looked out over the bay at tall-masted schooners, fast clipper ships, and slow barges.

Inside, the cottage was a bit dusty from lack of use. But Jeremy had stoked the wood-burning stove, and the rooms were warm. Another obvious attraction for Sammy was Bailey, who lay before the stove and thumped his tail against the wooden plank floor.

While the boy was distracted, Jeremy pulled Abbey into the bedroom they would soon share. Their lips met in soft, playful kisses that extended into long gentle explorations. Jeremy stroked her cheek, and Abbey ran her hands up against his shirt front feeling the taut muscles underneath.

"Have you made all the arrangements with Father William?" he asked.

"Yes, and I went for another fitting for my dress. It's almost finished."

"Mr. Rembold is going ta let me borrow a suit."

\*\*\*\*

On Saturday, Jeremy took Abbey on a tour of the island. They paced off the steps from the main house to the assistant's cottage. They paced the steps to the lighthouse. Soon, Abbey felt she knew every foot of the island. Sometimes, she held to Bailey's collar and let him assist her. The dog was a natural helper, concerned and gentle.

"The children at Pearson's loved him so," she said to Jeremy. "Perhaps he could come back with me to visit for a week? There's a child, Everett, who is deaf and blind. He's so locked into his own world. I think Bailey might be good for him."

"I'll miss him, but if ya think he can help, I'll let him go. What do ya say, Bailey, do ya want ta go back with Abbey?"

Bailey barked enthusiastically.

"He sounds like he understands what you say," Abbey said with a laugh.

"He does, every word," Jeremy teased.

Sunday afternoon as they stood again on the wharf awaiting the ferry, Jeremy locked her hand in his. "I love ya, Abbey, more and more each day."

"I love you too." She lifted her face to his for a deep and tender kiss, one that sent excitement coursing through her body.

Bailey was at her side and entered the ferry with her, though he cast a longing glance back at Jeremy.

All week, Abbey and Bailey worked with Everett. The boy learned to sign the words "dog," "tail," "ear," and "paw." He had fewer fits of rage and withdrew alone to himself less often.

Everett learned to throw a blue rubber ball, so that Bailey could retrieve it. They frolicked in the schoolyard behind the academy. They played in the snow, and Abbey heard Everett laugh for the first time when Bailey licked his face. The boy's appetite picked up, and he slept better at night.

The other children loved the dog too.

"No more treats for Bailey," Abbey warned as the children saved table scraps in napkins to feed the Lab later. "He's getting too fat."

The children giggled.

On the Friday morning that Abbey and Bailey were

to return to Little Brewster Island, the four children in her class helped her bathe the friendly Labrador in a copper tub. His coat was brushed out into a sleek ebony.

"He'll go home looking better than when he arrived," Ida said.

"You won't have to walk me today," Abbey said to Ida. "Bailey will be my guide and protector."

After lunch, she and the dog walked in the direction of the ferry landing. Abbey could tell from the way Bailey pulled on the leash that the dog needed to relieve himself. She let him go and heard him rush out into the park near the waterfront. Waiting, she braced herself against the cold sea air.

\*\*\*\*

Michael Gregory had been among the dock workers on the first Friday that Ida had walked Abbey to the ferry landing, but he'd been too busy pilfering a china plate with a gold rim to take much notice.

*It's so damn hard to make a living, a man's got to do whatever he can to get a leg up.*

The man next to him jabbed him with a pointed elbow.

"Here she comes again." The worker's breath reeked of whiskey.

"Who?"

"That good-looking girl from last week."

Gregory looked up from the loading dock. Abbey was crossing the park. She carried a purse and a new carpetbag. He also quickly assessed that, if he were to walk on the other side of a hedge of hawthorn roses, no one would see his approach.

"I'm going to take a quick break," he told the

foreman, a man with a grizzly beard and a lazy eye.

"Don't be long about it, or I'll dock your pay," he growled.

Gregory moved down the gangplank and made a sharp left, strolling in the direction of the park. As soon as possible, he ducked behind the hedge which sheltered him from the view of the docks. He fingered the cold steel blade in his pocket. He looked left and right. No one was in sight.

As he neared Abbey, he reached out and grasped her wrist.

"Don't scream unless you want to be stabbed in the side," he warned. "'And me the purse. If you say one word, I'll finish off one of those pathetic children at your school."

A black Lab raced toward him barking and growling. It knocked him to the ground.

"Get off me, you damn dog!"

A policeman's shrill whistle blew, high and piercing. Michael drew his knife and sank it into the dog's side releasing a flow of warm, sticky blood. Bailey yelped.

"After him!"

Two police officers lifted Gregory from the ground and handcuffed his arms behind his back. Gregory spit on the ground.

"That mangy cur attacked me!"

"We saw you grab the lady's purse," said one of the officers. "The dog just got to you before we could. Take him to the jail, Alcott."

The second officer jerked Gregory forward.

\*\*\*\*

"Ma'am, I'm Tom O'Reilly. Is this your purse?"

Abbey felt for it with a trembling hand. "Yes," she said. "That man, Gregory, has stolen from me before."

"I'm Officer Tom O'Reilly, and he's being arrested and taken to the jail by Officer Alcott. You need to accompany us to give a statement."

"But I'm supposed to catch the ferry."

"We've got to have your information in order to hold him. You must press charges."

"My dog. Where is the dog?"

"He's been stabbed in the side," the officer said. "I'll help you get him proper care." He finally noticed Abbey was blind and fetched her cane from the hedge where it had fallen.

"Take me to him," she said, her eyes filling with tears.

He led her to the injured animal lying on his side and licking his own wound.

Abbey knelt. "Oh, Bailey." She touched his side and felt the sticky blood and heard a soft whimper. Tears rolled down her cheeks.

\*\*\*\*

Jeremy paced the dock on Little Brewster and checked his pocket watch again. He squinted his eyes, and finally he saw the ferry bumping over the choppy surf. Sam moseyed down from the lighthouse and joined him.

As the launch grew closer, Jeremy recognized Carrie Rembold who had ridden it over to Boston earlier to complete some shopping. He didn't see Abbey at all.

Sam helped tie the ferry to the dock when the captain, Ezra Pichard, tossed the ropes over.

Carrie descended the gangplank. "Abbey never

boarded," she said.

"Something is wrong," Jeremy told Sam. "You've got ta let me go ta the mainland and find out what's happened ta her."

"We'll be shorthanded tonight, but you'd better check into things," the head keeper said.

"Can ya wait while I quickly pack a bag?" Jeremy asked the ferry Captain Pichard, a gray-haired salt with a weather-worn face and leathery skin.

"Sure, but be quick about it." Ezra held a pipe between yellowed teeth. The pungent scent of tobacco filled the air.

Jeremy raced up to the assistant's cottage and threw an extra set of clothes and a razor into his bag. Then he jogged to the wharf and boarded the transport.

*What's happened to Abbey?*

Was this boat always so slow? He longed to get to the city. When they finally arrived, he sprang from his seat and hurried over the gangplank. His first stop was Pearson Academy.

"But she left here at one thirty," Ida told him. "She had Bailey with her, so she felt safe enough without me."

"I don't know where ta look for her," Jeremy said, but then a loud rap sounded at the front door, and Matron Bards let Abbey and a uniformed policeman inside. The officer doffed his hat and entered the foyer.

"I'm Officer O'Reilly, and I'm returning Miss Morrison. I'm afraid she's had a bit of a scare."

"Abbey!" Jeremy embraced her. "What happened?"

"Why don't we all sit down in the parlor," invited Matron Bards who saw that Abbey seemed weak in the knees.

Ida followed them and watched her friend sink down on the narrow rose-colored sofa.

"It was Michael Gregory again," Abbey said. Her ashen face and trembling hands revealed her torment.

"Aye, but this time we've caught him, and he's locked in a cell until a trial can be arranged," said the officer.

"He snatched my purse, and I recognized his voice. But it was Bailey who brought him down."

"That dog's a hero to be sure," said O'Reilly.

"Oh Jeremy..." Abbey's voice faltered, and tears gushed. "Bailey was stabbed. We've taken him to a horse doctor, who has sewn up the wound. If anything happens to Bailey, I'll never forgive myself."

"At the moment, I'm more concerned about you," Jeremy said. "Are you hurt?"

"No." She shook her head. "I went to the station with Officer O'Reilly, and I gave testimony against Mr. Gregory on both counts."

"Of course, we'll expect her to appear at his trial. But this time, he should be put away for a while. He's been brought in before as a suspect in a thievery ring that pawns items at various shops in the surrounding area, but we didn't have enough evidence to convict him. And don't worry, he doesn't have enough money to post bail."

"I'll bring in some tea to steady your nerves," Matron Bards said and exited.

"I've got to return to the station," O'Reilly said. "But I'll be back in touch with you as soon as I know when a trial is set."

"I'd like to get my hands on this Michael

Gregory," Jeremy said. Adrenaline rushed through his body, and he felt like striking someone.

"Just let the law handle this," the officer warned. "Don't want to get in trouble as a vigilante."

"Abbey, you must have been so scared," Ida said.

"I'm glad they caught him. I've been upset about losing Jeremy's wedding band and love spoon."

"I'll carve ya another," he promised. "Now where is this horse doctor? I'd like ta go check on Bailey."

Jeremy found Bailey in a horse stall filled with clean hay at a livery stable on the south end of the common just as Abbey had described. The dog lifted his weary head when Jeremy entered but did not try to stand. He whimpered a little but beat his tail welcomingly against the floor.

"He's taken some water," said a young groom, Arthur Winslow. "He did really well when the doc stitched him up."

"I hope infection doesn't set in," Jeremy said.

He knelt down and scratched Bailey's head and ears. Then he unwrapped a bit of chopped liver he'd purchased from a butcher and let the dog lick it up.

"Doc Branson knows his way with animals. The dog will be right as rain in a few weeks. Don't you worry. Right as rain."

Chapter Sixteen

"Oh Ida, I dread testifying in that trial. What if the jury doesn't believe me?" Abbey asked.

"They will."

"And it's my fault that Bailey was wounded. What if he dies? That will be my fault too."

"Calm down. Have faith," Ida said. "Let's go get the children and practice math. They are in music now."

When they had retrieved the children, Ida brought out an abacus and sat down with Molly and Lucy.

"What is two and two?" she asked, sliding the beads as she spoke. She let Molly feel the beads.

"Four," the child said.

Everett sought out Abbey and spelled dog into her hand.

Abbey knew he did not have sufficient vocabulary for her to explain. She let him feel her hand. She brought her fingers to her thumb quickly, the sign for "no."

Everett grabbed her arms and shook her, rage evident in his tight grip. His insistent fingers bruised her skin, but she knew he didn't understand.

"I miss him too," she said aloud.

When Jeremy returned from the livery stable, Matron Bards graciously invited him to stay for dinner, beef stew and collards, and offered him the settee in the parlor to stay the night. Abbey brought him a blue wool blanket.

"I've got to go back tomorrow. You'll come with me?" Jeremy's warm hand sought hers.

"Do you think Bailey will be okay?" she asked. "I'm so sorry."

"I think so. It's not your fault," Jeremy reassured. "He just needs rest and time to heal."

"Before we leave tomorrow, I want you to meet Father William," Abbey said.

After breakfast next morning, they walked to St. James's and found the priest in the sanctuary. It had been years since Jeremy had been in a church, and the high arched ceiling, the stained glass windows, and flickering votive candles evoked comforting memories.

"Father William, this is Jeremy," Abbey said with pride.

The gray-haired priest in his cassock extended his arm, and the two men shook hands.

"Have a seat, both of you," he invited. "Abbey told me you have family arriving in March."

"Yes."

"Then I need to prepare you for the conditions they may have endured since you left Ireland. The famine has killed thousands. I've heard of mass graves where men, women, and children are dumped unceremoniously. With poor nutrition, diseases spread: cholera, pneumonia, and scurvy. Sometimes when the ships arrive, they are quarantined if disease on board is epidemic. The ship will be anchored in the harbor, and passengers will be kept aboard until they can be examined by doctors and cleared."

"I've told Abbey about the coffin ships," Jeremy said. "I experienced them first hand. I remember well the ache of starvation."

"It's especially hard on the very young and the elderly. I will pray for your family." The priest stood. A brass cross on a chain rested against his black robe.

"Thank you, Father. I'll light a candle before I leave."

That afternoon they crossed to the island on the ferry.

Over the weekend, Abbey and Carrie became fast friends. Abbey helped her with the boys, the baking, and the laundry. On Saturday afternoon before he went up to the lantern room, Jeremy entertained them with his fiddle. He played ballads, reels, and hymns. The Rembold children clapped along. But as the sky grew dusky, he left to man the light. For a little while, Abbey stayed in the lantern room with him enjoying his warm embrace and gentle kisses.

"I'm afraid I'm going ta have ta send you down," Jeremy said. "You are way too much of a distraction, in a very good way. But I can't have any calamities at sea. Not on my watch. You understand, don't you?"

"Yes," Abbey said with a smile. "But I'll miss you."

She descended the stairs and returned to the Rembolds' house to help Carrie mend the boys' clothes. Her new friend was astonished at how well she could sew.

"Your stitches are straighter and smaller than mine," she said.

"It took a lot of practice," Abbey said, "but then I probably had fewer distractions."

"I never enjoyed sewing," Carrie confided. "I was always pricking a finger, usually my thumb. You make it look so easy, and you're much faster. I see the way that you're making more than one stitch at a time."

"I can't tell you how many times I heard my aunt repeat the proverb, a stitch in time saves nine." Abbey giggled.

"Well, it's nice to have company doing the darning. Sammy especially is hard on his clothes. Little hooligan. And I'm trying to save his clothes for his brother."

**\*\*\*\***

In Boston, light snow drifted down on the dark brick building that was the city jail.

"You've got a visitor," a guard barked.

A filthy stevedore who smelled of sweat and urine shuffled up to the bars of Michael Gregory's dim and dusty cell. Benjamin Morton had been Gregory's accomplice on several of the dock thefts.

"Got yourself in a pickle this time," Ben grunted with a grimace that revealed a missing front tooth.

"Did ya just come 'ere to gloat?" Gregory snarled.

The bored guard leaned back against the corridor wall eyeing them suspiciously.

"No, the boss sent me to tell you, you've been sacked."

In a low mumble only Benjamin could decipher, Gregory said, "Kill the blind girl."

Morton gave a slight nod.

"Time's up," the guard said and hustled Ben down the hallway.

**\*\*\*\***

Jeremy insisted on going back with Abbey on Sunday afternoon. "I'm taking no more chances," he declared. He walked her to Pearson's and kissed her gently inside the foyer. "Till Friday," he whispered hoarsely.

"Till Friday," she echoed.

She heard the door open and listened to his footsteps departing down the outside steps. The exaltation she always felt in his presence deflated to loss and desolation.

*The children will cheer me up.*

With Ida's help, she sought out Everett. Jeremy had carved a six-holed flute for him. She had read that some deaf children could sometimes feel the vibrations of music and rhythm. Patiently, she taught him how to finger the holes and blow gently.

Lucy and Molly played with the doll Abbey had made Lucy for Christmas, and Abbey realized she needed to make another one for Molly. She had leftover skeins of brown wool for hair. After the children went to bed, Abbey stayed awake and prayed for Jeremy's mother and brother, who no doubt tossed somewhere upon the Atlantic.

*How courageous they must be. Will they like me?*

She tossed and turned a while before falling asleep.

\*\*\*\*

Before he returned to the dock to take the ferry back to the island, Jeremy detoured to St. James's. He found Father William and asked if he might enter the confessional. "It's been years since I've had the opportunity," Jeremy explained.

From behind the black curtain, the priest listened to Jeremy's thoughts and feelings.

"For a long time, I've thought the scar on my face was allowed by God ta give me the mark of Cain, the first man ta murder his brother. I'm not sure how many men I killed in the war, but there are two that haunt me."

"If you had not killed these men, wouldn't they have killed you?"

"Probably. I don't know. I'll never know."

"God is merciful. The Lord says that if you confess your sins, he will forgive them. I understand that you're a light keeper now, and you work to save men's lives."

"Sometimes I fail at that as well."

"Devote yourself to prayer and the reading of the gospels, for God alone is able to cleanse us of all unrighteousness."

\*\*\*\*

On Wednesday, Abbey went for the final fitting of her wedding dress, and Ida accompanied her.

"You look absolutely glowing," her friend said. "Your skin is like fine bone china with just a blush of pink on your cheeks. Your eyes are sparkling like the sun on the ocean."

"What should I do with my hair?" Abbey asked.

"I know how to make a French braid," Laura, the dressmaker, said. "I'll teach you, Ida."

She quickly loosened Abbey's silky hair from the tight bun at the base of her slender neck. The auburn tresses fell almost to her waist, thick and wavy. Then she skillfully separated the hair and began to braid. A few loose tendrils framed Abbey's face.

"I have some white flowers made of cloth to intersperse in the braid," Laura said and went to the back room to fetch them. When she returned, she handed the blossoms to Ida who worked them into the braid. Then both women drew back to survey their handiwork.

"Perfect," said Miss Brooks. "And now the veil." She settled it over Abbey's hair and face.

"Jeremy is going to be amazed," Ida said.

After the fitting, the two women went to Simon's livery to check on Bailey. Fawn-colored Jerseys grazed on the common where a few green shoots heralded the coming of early spring even though frost glistened on the surface. Abbey and Ida walked arm and arm together.

"That's strange," Ida said in a low voice.

"What?" Abbey asked.

"There's a man that I saw yesterday on the corner. He was watching us when we took the children outside. At least, I think it's the same man."

"It is times like this when I miss being sighted the most," Abbey replied. "I have no idea what dangers are out there. It never mattered in Arbor where everyone knew everyone else. But here, in such a bustling city, there are so many strangers. What does he look like?"

"He's smoking like a chimney and missing his left front tooth. But don't worry. People are everywhere. In fact, there's a police officer strolling the perimeter of the common near the North Church."

Abbey heard carriages passing and pedestrians talking. Soon, they ducked inside the livery stable out of the wind and nippy air. Abbey smelled the pungent hay and the sweat of horses. She heard the crunching of oats being devoured. She counted the stalls to reach Bailey.

"Oh, good. He's standing," Ida said. "Feelin' better, boy?"

The dog walked stiffly forward, not his usual rambunctious self but wagging his tail in greeting.

Abbey knelt and let him lick her face.

"Maybe you can go home soon," she told him.

\*\*\*\*

"Abbey," Matron Bards called from the door of the classroom. When Abbey approached her, the head of the school told her in a low, confidential tone, "Officer O'Reilly is here to speak to you."

Abbey reached out for the matron's arm and went with her to the office.

"Miss Morrison, I have brought someone to speak to you." Abbey recognized O'Reilly's voice. Like Jeremy's it had a slight Irish brogue. "This is Wilham Anderson, the attorney who will prosecute Michael Gregory. He needs to depose you. The trial is set for the twenty-fourth of February."

With trembling limbs, Abbey sat down and arranged her long skirt around her.

"I want you to go over both of your encounters with Michael Gregory to the best of your memory," Anderson said.

"I hate to think about it." Abbey shuddered.

"The more times we go over your story, the more comfortable you will be in the witness box."

Biting her lower lip, Abbey nodded. She retold the story of her escape on the road from Portland to Arbor, gave details of her nights in the forest, and relived her fear of being recaptured.

"How did you know that the man who attacked you near the Boston docks on the twenty-ninth of January was the same man when you cannot see, Miss Morrison?"

*He doesn't believe me. Isn't he supposed to be on my side?* "I recognized his voice."

"You expect a jury to believe that?"

"Yes!" She wilted into tears.

"I really don't think you should distress her like this," Matron Bards snapped in indignation.

"Miss Morrison, I do apologize," he said. "Of course, I believe your story, but you must realize that the defense attorney will do whatever he can to cast doubt upon your testimony. You must steel your emotions and stand up for yourself. Give good, logical reasons. Now try again. How did you recognize his voice?"

"The blind develop an acute sense of hearing and smell," she said. "I could smell cigar tobacco and alcohol on his breath. His accent has a touch of London cockney.

He drops the *H* sound at the beginning of words. He himself made reference to our earlier encounter." She spoke with more assurance and conviction.

"Much better," the lawyer praised. "Don't let the defense bully or rattle you."

Abbey nodded, but she still found it difficult to relax. The last thing she wanted was for Michael Gregory to be acquitted and released.

Chapter Seventeen

"I've been down to Hodgkin's Shipping Company, and they expect the *Atlantic Voyager* any day now," Jeremy told Abbey on Friday as they walked from Pearson's back to the ferry landing. "I haven't seen Mam or Shawn in five years. They will see how I've changed." His tone betrayed his anxiety.

"They've probably changed as well," she said. "It may be awkward at first."

"But you don't need to worry. They will both like you," Jeremy said.

"I hope so. Harry Winslow said Bailey should rest another week, but next Friday you can take him back to the island."

"I went to see him on my way to pick you up," Jeremy said. "He's getting back to his old self."

They crossed the gangplank to the ferry, and Jeremy helped the captain cast off. As the boat bounced on the choppy surf, Jeremy shielded Abbey from the wind. In the harbor, he could make out a three-masted ship with billowing white sails. As it drew closer, he read aloud the name *Atlantic Voyager.*

"There she is!" Jeremy exclaimed.

"Please," he begged the captain, "can we pull closer? My mother and brother are supposed to be on board!"

"That shouldn't throw us off schedule," the captain

replied with a smile and steered in the direction of the passenger ship. When they were close, he sounded the fog horn, and the boatswain of the *Atlantic Voyager* walked leeward, leaned over the rail, and shouted down.

"Ahoy!"

With chin trained upward, Jeremy shouted back, "Are Mary and Shawn McKetcheon on board?"

"Aye! But so is cholera. We're sure to be quarantined. Are they relatives?"

"My mam and brother. Are they ill?"

"I'll fetch your brother."

The boatswain disappeared and soon reappeared with Shawn. Jeremy could barely recognize him beneath the scraggly beard and long, wildly curling hair. He looked like a bear. But Shawn waved his arms.

"Jeremy! Or do my eyes deceive me?"

"Are you well?"

"I'm good so far, but Mam is doing poorly. She can't come up in the wind. But she'll be glad to hear I saw you!"

"God bless you both. I'll come fetch you as soon as you're released. I'm the assistant keeper at Little Brewster Light here in the harbor. There was no time to write you before you left Ireland."

"This good news will surely bring her round!" He waved farewell as the ferry headed on toward the island.

\*\*\*\*

"Our days together always fly by," Abbey complained when Sunday afternoon arrived. Reluctant to leave, she had tried to savor every moment. Jeremy kissed her forehead.

"I know," he said. "I miss ya something turble during the week, but it won't be much longer. If I get word that the *Atlantic Voyager* is debarking, I'll be in ta see you this week."

"Everett liked the flute," Abbey said. "I'm afraid the rest of us sometimes cover our ears when he plays. Ida and I took him to Bailey which greatly reassured him. I think he understands now Bailey was hurt but is recuperating. Bailey licked his hands, and Everett laughed. It was a wonder to hear."

"You and Ida be careful going out alone," Jeremy warned.

"We will. I'm nervous about the trial. I'll be glad to put it behind me next week."

"I'll be there Friday when it starts, ta give you strength. I wish you didn't have ta go through all this. But we'll all feel safer when Michael Gregory is locked up for good."

Each day as the trial drew closer, Abbey became more anxious. At night, she tossed and turned, unable to get comfortable. After she ate, she experienced heartburn, and she noticed that she snapped at the children when they disobeyed.

"You're not yourself this week," Ida noted.

"No, I'm sorry. I hate to think about testifying Friday."

Ida squeezed her hand to reassure her. "We'll be there to sustain you."

Late in the afternoon on Wednesday, Abbey decided to cross the common to visit Bailey. The dog jumped on her affectionately and capered about the stall.

"He's much better," Harry said. "Full of energy."

"Good, because Jeremy's ready to take him home."

"Can't say I won't miss him," Harry replied. "It's easy to grow fond of him."

Abbey left the livery tapping her cane back and forth across the well-known path traversing the common.

Suddenly, a rough, calloused hand grabbed her upper arm, and a voice rasped in her ear. "Don't cry out. I have a knife to your back."

Abbey's blood froze. The sharp point of the blade pricked her spine. The voice did not belong to Michael Gregory—too low and nasal. All at once, the shrill of a policeman's whistle sounded and the thud of running footfalls. Her assailant released her wrist and fled.

"Halt!" shouted an officer. Several men raced past her, followed by a string of curses. She stood trembling, afraid to move.

"Are you all right? I'm Officer Connors."

"I'm Abigail Morrison, but who was that man?"

"Two other officers are chasing him now."

"Please can we go inside the livery stable? I'd feel more at ease there."

"Of course."

They made their way back to the warm barn with its series of stalls. Before long, the two police officers who had run after the stranger returned breathing heavily.

"We lost him. Don't know how he got away," said one, who introduced himself as James Lance.

"My friend, Ida Allen, said she thought a man was watching us several days ago. She said he was missing his left front tooth."

"So was this man," Lance said, trying to catch his

breath.

"Did you recognize him?" Officer Connors asked.

"No."

"Aren't you the young woman who was assaulted by Michael Gregory, whose trial starts Friday?" Connors asked.

"Yes," Abigail replied.

"I think we should check around the docks and ask some questions after we take Miss Morrison home."

"But what did he want?" Abbey stammered.

"Probably wants to stop your testimony at the trial. Did he threaten you?"

"Yes. He said he had a knife."

"Some wharf rat. But don't you worry, we'll track him down."

\*\*\*\*

Jeremy arrived early Friday morning to escort Abbey to the Boston Courthouse on Court Square. Four solid columns held up the portico. As he helped her up the steps, he spoke softly. "I have good news. A doctor has cleared Mam and Shawn. I'll meet them at Bayview General Hospital tomorrow."

"I'm so glad," Abbey replied. "Now we have something to look forward to other than this wretched trial."

Even Abbey could sense the intensity in the courtroom as they entered. She sat down next to Jeremy and tried to calm herself by taking in deep breaths and slowly releasing them. She listened as the bailiff told them all to rise. Like everyone else, Abbey stood in respect as the judge entered the courtroom.

"The Honorable Justice Seagraves presiding," the bailiff announced.

"You may be seated," said the deep bass voice of the judge. "We are here today to decide the guilt or innocence of Michael Gregory, who is charged with two counts of theft and one charge of assault. Will the defendant please stand?"

Abbey heard a chair slide back.

"Mr. Rogers, how does your client plea?"

"Not guilty, Your 'Onor," Gregory said.

She recognized the belligerent voice and quivered.

"Mr. Wilham Anderson is representing the city of Boston," the judge continued. "Mr. Anderson, you may make your opening statement."

"I intend to prove that Michael Gregory has stolen property from Miss Abigail Morrison on two separate occasions, once on the road from Portland to Arbor in Maine in late December of last year and again on January 29th of this year on the common near the Boston docks. On both occasions, he attempted to assault Miss Morrison, who is blind. In Maine, he left her in a wilderness area during a severe snowstorm. In Boston, he also threatened her with violence, held her at knife point, and stabbed a black Labrador retriever that intervened. The dog prevented further violence against Abigail Morrison and was seriously injured but not killed."

"Mr. Rogers, will you please address the court?"

"Gentlemen of the jury, the defendant, Michael Gregory, is not guilty. He offered to transport Miss Morrison from Portland to Arbor, but when she refused to pay him, he demanded that she give him a gold ring to hold as collateral until she reimbursed him for his time and effort. She panicked and ran from him leaving her bags. When he encountered her again in Boston to collect payment, she had her dog attack him, and to prevent the vicious beast from tearing open his neck, he acted in self-defense."

"What a lie," Abigail said in a low tone to Jeremy. He squeezed her hand. There were murmurs throughout the courtroom.

The judge rapped his gavel.

"There will be no comments from the spectators. Mr. Anderson, call your first witness."

"I call Abigail Morrison to the stand."

Abbey stood. Her knees felt weak. With the cane swinging down the aisle, there was not another sound but its tapping.

The bailiff stood before her and guided her hand to the Bible. "Do you swear to tell the truth, the whole truth, and nothing but the truth?"

"I do," Abbey said.

He led her to the witness box where she sat down.

"Miss Morrison, will you please tell us where you were on December 27th, 1869" Anderson asked.

"I left Boston on the six a.m. train to Portland, Maine, and arrived there at 1:10 p.m. I asked the ticket seller if he knew a reliable driver for me to get to Arbor where I have a home. A man, who later introduced himself as Michael Gregory, offered to take me there free of charge. He said he was headed in that direction."

"Then what happened?"

"We drove out of Portland for approximately forty-five minutes. I was wearing a gold band on a chain around my neck. It was a wedding band for my betrothed. I had it inscribed with the words 'All my love.' Suddenly, Mr. Gregory tore it from my neck."

Murmurs arose in the courtroom.

"Did you ask for the ring back?"

"I don't know. I was startled and terrified. Then he forced his lips on mine. I pushed him away, jumped down, and swatted the mule to make it run. I fled back down the road toward Portland, climbed an embankment, and hid in the forest."

"Was there any other personal property that Michael Gregory took?"

"My bag with my clothes and my purse were left in the wagon."

"What was the weather like that day?"

"Snow and ice. Freezing temperatures. I hid for two days and nights."

"How did you survive?" Anderson's voice exuded empathy to arouse sympathy from the jury.

"I took shelter under my thick wool coat and ate ice."

"Were you afraid that you might freeze to death?"

"Yes. I also felt threatened by wolves."

"How were you rescued?" the attorney asked.

"My betrothed, Jeremy McKetcheon, learned I'd left Boston but had not arrived in Arbor. He and two other men found me and brought me back to Portland."

"When did you encounter Michael Gregory again?"

"Jeremy—Mr. McKetcheon—and I were returning to Boston by train, and I heard Mr. Gregory's voice on the train."

"How did you know it was him?"

"I can hear very well, and I recognized the timbre of his voice and his Cockney accent."

"Did he see you?"

"I don't think so, but I can't be sure."

"Why did you return to Boston?" Anderson asked.

"To resume my job at the Pearson Academy for the Blind where I am a teacher."

"Now please tell us about January 29th. What happened on that day?"

"I was on my way to the ferry landing, when Mr. Gregory grabbed me and threatened me at knife point to hand over my purse."

"I object!" shouted Mr. Rogers. "The witness cannot see. She does not know who grabbed her."

"Sustained," said the judge. "Please rephrase your question, Mr. Anderson."

"How do you know that the man who grabbed you was Mr. Gregory?"

"I heard him speak. Then our dog, Bailey, who had wandered off, returned and wrestled him to the ground. After that, the police arrested Mr. Gregory."

"Thank you, Miss Morrison."

"Mr. Rogers, you may cross-examine the witness."

"Yes, Your Honor, and I would like to remind the witness that you are under oath."

Abigail nodded.

"Miss Morrison, do you believe that Michael Gregory is the only man in Boston with a Cockney accent?" Rogers asked in a booming bass voice dripping with sarcasm.

A few giggles erupted in the courtroom, but they were quickly stifled by a glare from the judge. Abbey's face grew hot.

"No, I do not. There are other distinctive qualities to his voice."

"Still, you did not see Mr. Gregory. You did not see anything, did you?"

"I object!" Anderson was on his feet.

"Sustained," growled the judge like a bulldog with its back up. "Mr. Rogers, approach the bench."

When the defense lawyer obeyed, Judge Seagraves warned him.

"Another comment like that, and I will charge you with contempt. You will not badger the witness."

"Yes, Your Honor."

"The court will recess until one o'clock," the judge announced. "You may step down, Miss Morrison."

People filed out, but Jeremy stepped forward to assist Abbey. "Let's go ta Katie's Restaurant next door and eat," he said.

"Am I making a fool of myself?" she asked.

"No, Rogers is a bag of hot air, and everyone knows it."

They walked to Katie's and sat at a table for two where Jeremy read the menu aloud to Abbey.

"I'll try the clam chowder," she said, "but I doubt if it will be as good as yours."

Chapter Eighteen

When the trial resumed, Anderson brought Officer O'Reilly to the stand. The policeman testified he saw Bailey knock Michael Gregory to the ground.

"Then the defendant stabbed the dog, and when we arrested him, he had Miss Morrison's purse inside his vest."

"Thank you, Mr. O'Reilly."

"Mr. Rogers, do you have any questions for Officer Reilly?"

"Not at this time."

"Mr. Rogers, will you please call your first witness?"

"I call Michael James Gregory."

The defendant swaggered to the bailiff and was sworn in.

"Mr. Gregory, will you please tell the jury where you were on January 29<sup>th</sup> of this year."

"I'm a stevedore and was taking a break, when I saw a blind woman walk by. I watched 'er, and she was accosted by a man who grabbed 'er purse. I chased after 'im. 'E threw down the purse, and I retrieved it. I was about to return it when this black beast of a dog attacked me. And that's God's 'onest truth."

"Then what happened?"

"I was arrested and hauled off to jail. I lost my job, and I'm on trial. That's my payback for being a Good

Samaritan."

"Prior to January 29<sup>th</sup> had you ever seen Miss Morrison before?"

"Once. I offered her a ride to Arbor at the fare of two dollars."

"And did she pay you?"

"She did not. More than 'alfway there, she told me she couldn't pay."

"Then what happened?"

"I asked her for collateral, something to 'old until she made good on 'er debt. She 'anded me a wedding band."

"Thank you, Mr. Gregory."

"Mr. Anderson, would you like to question Mr. Gregory."

"Yes, Your Honor."

"Mr. Gregory, let me remind you that you are still under oath and that there is a heavy penalty for perjury."

Gregory nodded. "I don't need reminding." He sneered. "It's my word against 'ers."

"The wedding band you took from Miss Morrison. What do you estimate it is worth?"

"I 'ave no idea."

"Come on, make a guess. Was it solid gold?"

"Mighta been."

"But certainly it was worth more than two dollars. I have here a receipt for the ring Miss Morrison wore around her neck, stating its value at seventy-five dollars." He showed Gregory the paper and then handed it to the judge.

"Where is that ring now?" Anderson asked.

"I don't know. I pawned it because she never paid

me."

"And what amount did you receive for that ring?"

"Ten, twenty dollars."

"Where did you pawn the ring?"

"I don't remember."

"Come on, Mr. Gregory, it was less than two months ago."

"I said I don't remember."

"What time did you and Miss Morrison arrive in Arbor?"

"We never did. She got all 'ysterical, jumped down, and ran off."

"So you never even completed the trip for which Miss Morrison was supposed to pay you $2.00, yet you kept a $75.00 ring. Did you have any of her other possessions?"

"Like I said she run off like a rabbit. I thought maybe she was crazy."

"What other possessions did you have?"

"Some old carpetbag and a worn-out purse."

"And did you return these items to Miss Morrison?"

"I never 'ad a chance. I told you, she run off."

"Then do you still have her satchel and purse?"

"No, sir."

"Why not?"

"What am I going to do with a lady's purse and old bag?" He guffawed.

A few of his cronies in the courtroom laughed as well.

Judge Seagraves rapped his gavel. "If there are any more outbursts, I'll have the courtroom cleared."

Anderson approached the bench. "Your Honor, I

have the employment records of Michael Gregory with Hadley and Sons. I enter these as evidence that Michael Gregory did not come to work on December 27th or 28th of last year."

Then the prosecutor turned to Gregory. "Can you please explain these absences?" Anderson asked.

"Yes, sir, I was sick."

"Did you see a doctor?"

"No, who can afford a doctor?"

"Is there a friend or relative who can vouch for your illness?"

"No, I tell you I 'ad a fever, and no one to nurse me."

"Yet you were not too ill to drive the road from Portland to Arbor in freezing temperatures."

"I object!" said Rogers. "That is not a question."

"Sustained," said Seagraves.

"Mr. Gregory, are you aware that Hadley and Sons have had complaints from shipping companies about items missing from their inventories?"

"I've 'eard rumors of such. It's a pity if it's true."

"I object!" Rogers stood. "These questions have nothing to do with Miss Morrison or the charges against my client."

"Your Honor," said Anderson, "I believe that this question does relate to Mr. Gregory's character."

"You must stick to the charges in this case," Seagraves ruled.

"Then I have no more questions at this time."

\*\*\*\*

The next morning, Anderson called Mr. Carl Peterson to the stand, and the witness was duly sworn. Peterson sat down and looked nervously at the crowd in the courtroom. He combed the fingers of his right hand through his thinning black hair and then rubbed his chin, his fidgeting an obvious sign of nerves.

"Would you please tell us where you live and what you do for a living?" Anderson queried.

"To be sure. I'm from Portland, Maine, and I run a store there."

"Mr. Peterson, do you recognize the man in this photograph?"

"Yes, sir. He said his name was Michael Gregory."

"And do you see him in this courtroom?"

"That's him sittin' over yonder." Peterson pointed at the defendant.

"And how do you know Michael Gregory?"

"He comes in the store now and again and trades items to me."

"When was the last time you saw him?"

"Second week of January."

"And did he trade with you that day?"

"Yep, he did." Peterson pulled two items from his coat pocket. "This carved wooden spoon and this gold wedding band he said belonged to him."

Abigail sucked in her breath and gripped Jeremy's hand.

"Mr. Peterson, will you please read the initials carved on the back of the spoon?"

"J.M."

"Now will you read the initials on the wood carving of this dog."

"The same, J.M."

"Do they look similar?"

"Yes, sir."

"The dog was carved by Jeremy McKetcheon who

is betrothed to Miss Morrison. Would you please read the inscription on the inside of the ring?"

Peterson squinted. "It says, 'With all my love, Abbey.' "

The spectators murmured.

The judge silenced them with a rap of his gavel. "Do you wish to cross examine, Mr. Rogers?"

"No, the defense rests."

\*\*\*\*

The jury deliberated only ten minutes before returning a guilty verdict. Abbey felt tension ease from her body until Gregory jumped from his seat.

"It's a damn lie. I'm innocent!"

The judge slammed the gavel down and ordered two uniformed police officers,

"Bring that man before the bench."

The officers each grabbed Gregory by his upper arms and propelled him forward.

"Michael Gregory, you are sentenced to ten years in prison for the charges against you and five additional years for perjury," Seagraves pronounced. "Take him back to the jail."

Gregory was led from the court.

As the spectators filed out, the judge called Abbey to the bench and handed her the love spoon and wedding band. "I believe these belong to you." He smiled.

"You have no idea how glad I am, for sentimental reasons, to get them back."

Jeremy led her outside. "Now that the trial is behind us, are you ready ta meet my family?" Jeremy asked.

"Absolutely," Abbey said.

"They're being held at Bayview General Hospital but have passed their physical examinations. Mam had bronchitis but is doing much better. Shawn has shaved and cut his hair. He looks like himself again."

"Let's go now," Abbey said. "I'm anxious to get to know them."

Jeremy took her arm and led the way.

****

An imposing building of brick and mortar with large columns, Bayview General Hospital stood on a bustling corner across from the Charles River. As Abbey and Jeremy walked the corridors, they passed crowded wards where cot after cot lined the walls. Some patients gave deep, hacking coughs. Others moaned quietly or thrashed in their sleep. Nurses scurried about with bedpans and trays. The smell of antiseptics made Jeremy gag.

"If you're not sick when ya come here, ya may be before ya leave," he said, breaking into a cold sweat.

Memories of his own time in the military hospital washed over him like a tidal wave. He saw again the amputated arms and legs tossed onto the gurneys. The agonized screams of the wounded echoed in his mind. He gripped Abbey's hand tighter.

"What's the matter?" she whispered. "Is something wrong?" He had stopped walking, and his shirt was damp with sweat.

"I need to sit down," he said. "I feel faint."

"Jeremy, what haunts you? What do you see?"

"The hospital during the war."

"You're trembling."

He staggered against her. A nurse noticed his distress, and with Abbey's help, she led him to a chair.

"Put your head between your knees. You're very pale," she said.

Jeremy obeyed, feeling nauseated.

"Now take some deep breaths and let the air out slowly. I'm going to fetch some water."

"You saw terrible things during the war," Abbey said. "But it's over. It's over."

Jeremy gulped in fresh air and then released it slowly, feeling his muscles relax as he did.

The nurse returned with a glass of water.

"Thank you," Jeremy said after sipping a few drops. "We're here to see Dr. William Jenkins. He's in charge of my family's health and immigration process."

"His office is at the end of the hall." The nurse, a young woman with red hair, smiled. "I'm Nora Corrigan, and I hope you're feeling better?"

"Yes," Jeremy said. "You might call it a fear of hospitals."

He stood and with Abbey's help walked down the hall, where they were greeted by Dr. Jenkins. The nurse followed.

"You look pale," the physician, a portly man with a receding hair line, noted.

"I'm not fond of hospitals," Jeremy said.

"You were in the war?" The doctor eyed him with empathy.

Jeremy nodded.

"So was I. Still have nightmares. Not all scars are visible," he said. "You're here to pick up your family, yes? I hope you will make an appointment to come see me, to talk about your fear of hospitals. I actually meet with a group of veterans once a month. We find that it helps to share our experiences."

"Does it meet in the hospital?"

Dr. Jenkins had to grin at the question. "You'll be relieved to know that it does not. Nora, will you fetch Shawn and Mary McKetcheon?"

"Of course," she said and exited.

"You've seen your brother, but not your mother, is that correct?"

"That's right, but my brother has told her about my—my appearance. So it won't be a shock to her." It suddenly dawned on him that he'd not properly introduced Abbey. "This is Abigail Morrison," he said, "the woman I'm engaged to marry."

"Miss Morrison, I'm pleased to meet you."

"Jeremy!" Shawn's voice boomed in the doorway. Jeremy stood. The brothers embraced, and then Jeremy took his petite mother in his arms. Her thin, frail body looked as limp as a ragdoll.

"Saints be praised. You're alive and well," she said. Her lively blue eyes sparkled. "It's good to hold my baby in my arms again."

She hugged him and then released him to give him an appraisal. Blue veins were visible beneath her paper-thin skin wrinkled with age. Her silver hair was swept back in a bun.

"Mam, this is Abbey." Pride glowed in Jeremy's eyes as a smile spread across his face.

"She's petite like me," Mary said. "And such a beauty. Aw look, I've brought a blush to her cheeks. I like a girl who's—"

"Modest," Jeremy and Shawn said together, finishing an oft-repeated remark.

"Well, I do," Mary chided. "Shawn told me of your awful ordeal. Is the trial over then?"

"Yes," Abbey said. "Michael Gregory will be behind bars for a long time. Not only was he found guilty, but I got back the wedding band and the love spoon Jeremy carved for me."

At the ferry landing, Mary McKetcheon pulled her dark shawl more closely around her. Bailey barked and paced the wharf as though he knew he was going home.

"I do dread to step foot upon a ship again," Mary said with a sigh.

"It's not a long ride." Abbey tried to put her at ease.

"And the water is calm today," Jeremy added.

"I told myself, I'd not get on another pitchin' vessel once I stepped foot on dry land again."

"Sit in the front and face the bow. You'll be fine," Jeremy said.

"I never learned ta swim like you lads," Mary confided.

"You've got a trained rescue worker right here." Shawn clapped Jeremy on the back.

As the ferry moved in, Jeremy assisted the captain by catching the ropes and tying them up to the dock. Shawn helped his mother across the gangplank, and Abbey sat next to her to calm her.

"I don't trust the sea," Mary said and gave an involuntary shiver.

"Have you thought about what you want ta do here?" Jeremy asked Shawn as they sat behind Mary and Abbey. Bailey rested at his feet.

"I've heard there's good farm land," he said, "not that we've any money ta purchase anything."

"There is. Abbey's uncle has a farm in Arbor. She also has a house there you could rent. Or you might be able ta get in the Light Keeping Service."

"I don't think that's for me. I'm not fond of the sea either. What does Abbey's uncle grow?"

"Blueberries and cranberries mostly. He raises chickens and sells eggs. Abbey's father raised hens as well. His flock is with her uncle now."

"I'd like ta do some carpentry on the side. You know I've always liked to build things."

"And you're good at it," Jeremy said.

Later on the island, Jeremy introduced his family to the Rembolds and took them to his cottage to eat. They feasted on hearty New England stew and relaxed before the fire.

"I'm going ta teach you how ta make Irish soda bread," Mary told Abbey.

"I'll look forward to it. I do like to bake."

"I need ta go take my shift with the light," Jeremy explained.

"I'll walk back up to the main house with you." Abbey stood.

Dusk shimmered along the horizon. One or two stars shone in the darkening sky. Sea gulls flapped away to their roosting places, and the roar of the waves as they splashed against the rocks seemed somehow comforting.

"I'm sorry the hospital brought back bad memories," Abbey said, taking his hand as they walked.

"'Tis better I'm feeling," he said. "Ever since I met ya."

"Still, it might be a good idea to go see Dr. Jenkins."

"I will." He stopped and turned her to him. Then cupping her chin in his calloused hand, he gently kissed her lips and stroked her cheek.

"I meant every word I had inscribed on your ring," Abbey said, and then standing on tiptoe, kissed him back, pressing her body against him.

**\*\*\*\***

A few days later at Abigail's prompting, Jeremy made a Wednesday appointment with Dr. Jenkins by sending a letter through the ferryboat captain. On the day of the appointment, he entered the office without much optimism. He sat down in a chair outside the examination room to wait until Nora ushered him inside.

Dr. Jenkins shook his hand heartily. "Good to see you again. I won't beat around the bush, Jeremy. I've treated many veterans who have scars from the war, and I've learned a little trick from reading about the French during the smallpox epidemic. Scarring to the face is difficult for many soldiers because it affects how they view themselves. Often they want to withdraw from others."

"That's because ya feel like a monster who frightens little children," Jeremy said. "You mentioned the French."

"Yes, the smallpox epidemic left terrible scarring, and the French used softened paraffin to put over the pox marks. Then they brushed on tinted powder to cover the wax."

"'Tis vanity, I know, but I would like ta look better on my wedding day even if Abbey canna see me."

"I thought we would try a little experiment," the doctor said. He kneaded some white paraffin between his thumb and forefinger. Then he applied it gently to Jeremy's scar, smoothing it over the skin and letting it harden. "I've mixed the powder with plant oils to give it a smooth texture. I'm going to use this small paint brush to apply it to your face."

"Not only a doctor, but an artist," Jeremy teased.

As a final step, Dr. Jeremy dusted dry powder over the surface to create a matte finish. "What do you think?" he asked as he offered Jeremy a hand mirror.

Jeremy looked at himself and smiled at the noticeable improvement. "You're a miracle worker sure 'nuff."

"I can teach you to apply it yourself. But a bit of a warning. It won't hold up to hot temperatures."

"Aye, my cheek will slide off my face, I imagine. Good that the New England temperatures are rarely hot."

"As I said before, not all scars visible. I've treated many veterans of the war. We have formed a group that meets informally once a month at the Episcopal Church. We've found that sharing some of what we experienced during the battles is, well, therapeutic. It helps to know that others are struggling with similar issues. I hope you'll join us. We're meeting this afternoon."

"I don't know," Jeremy said. "I try not ta think about the war. The atrocities I saw. The things we did."

"If you change your mind, we meet at the church across the street at seven o'clock. There's one other topic I wanted to address. I recently met a new doctor who specializes in eyes and eye surgery. I don't want to raise false hopes, but perhaps Abbey should let him examine her eyes. Some amazing progress has been made."

"I'll talk ta her, and thank you for your help."

"Would you like to come with me to the veteran's group I mentioned?"

"I'll try almost anything once."

"Some of the men have developed a problem with alcohol because they're trying to forget the past." Dr. Jenkins consulted his pocket watch. "They should be gathering in the Episcopal Church across the street pretty soon. Personally, I think it is better to confront the past that to run from it."

Jeremy walked with Jenkins through the hospital and across the street. The church was a round building with a low cone-shaped roof. A well-kept cemetery surrounded the sanctuary. Inside, men had gathered in the first two pews. Jeremy slid into one while Dr. Jenkins stood on the floor beneath the raised pulpit.

"Good afternoon, gentlemen. Let's open our time together with prayer." Like the others, Jeremy bowed his head.

"Oh Lord, the great healer, be with us and guide us. Let us experience wholeness and forgiveness through you. Amen.

"I'd like introduce you to a friend of mine, Jeremy McKetcheon. Like you, he is a veteran of the worst war our country has ever experienced. Like you, he is seeking peace from traumatic memories."

Jeremy stood, nodded awkwardly, and sat back down. He didn't want to draw attention to himself. The door at the back of the church opened, and a disheveled man stumbled up the aisle and slumped down on the second pew. Jeremy smelled whiskey and noted the man's red, bleary eyes.

"Good to see you, Billings," Dr. Jenkins said.

The man grunted.

"Does anyone want to open our discussion today?"

"Anybody here ever held at Andersonville Prison?" Billings asked with a slight slurring of speech. "It was hell on earth, I tell you. Hell on earth. Never knew men could get so hungry they'd fight over a dead rat and eat it raw. We looked like skeletons covered over with skin. Hot as hell too in that damn Georgia heat."

"During the potato blight, some people tried to eat grass," Jeremy said quietly.

"Puked it up too," a dark-haired gentleman said. "I'm Dermot Carmody, county Cork."

Jeremy bobbed his head in acknowledgement.

"Damndest thing," Billings continued as though never interrupted. "We had our little mascot there, drummer boy, fresh faced as a babe. When he died, and the guards prepared the body for burial, they discovered he was girl. Now why would a girl enlist in the army? Cut her hair short and everything?"

"I've shared before that I suffered a lot of guilt as a doctor working the field hospital. We often had to make tough choices about who to treat and who to let die. Triage, they called it. But we sometimes made the wrong decisions and lost both patients."

"We have to forgive ourselves," said a gangly young man. "Concentrate on the fact that the slaves got their freedom, and the Union was preserved."

"We have to forgive the Rebs too. They suffered as much as we did, maybe more since a lot of their homes were destroyed," said Dermot.

"You remind me of the Battle of Bull Run. After the fighting ended, we marauded some of the farms looking for food and supplies. We found a young woman in her kitchen where she had been baking bread.

She was dead on the floor with a hole in her chest from a stray bullet. Just a farmwife baking bread. Reminded me so much of my wife back at home."

Silence lingered in the room as each man faced his own demons. Then Dr. Jenkins ended their meeting with prayer.

Alone in the tower with the glow of the light behind him and the expanse of the ocean before him, Jeremy pondered the agonizing memories the men had shared. He realized he was not the only one to suffer guilt and occasional despair. He'd learned of one veteran who had killed himself.

But he did not wish to linger on unhappy thoughts like some old man on his death bed. He deliberately turned his attention to thoughts of Abbey, her radiant smile, her optimistic outlook. What would she think of his scarred face if she were cured of blindness? *I can't let selfishness stand in her way. Still, what if she gets her hopes up and the doctor can't help her? I have to let her decide.*

****

"Only ten days until the wedding," Abbey told Ida as they watched the children on the playground. "Saturday, March 26th, at St. James's. My aunt and uncle arrive on the twenty-fourth."

"How are the instructions in Catholic theology with Father William going?"

"Very well. He's a good teacher. But something else is bothering me a bit."

"What do you mean?"

"Jeremy mentioned a doctor here in Boston has done some successful eye operations that have restored the sight of his patients."

"That's wonderful," Ida said.

"I can't help wondering, though, if Jeremy mentioned this because my blindness bothers him. Maybe he's having second thoughts about marrying a woman who can't see."

"I don't think so, Abbey." Ida shook her head in dismissal. "But how do you feel about a cure?"

"I've never expected to see. It would be miraculous to look one day at my own child's face. But I don't know how painful or costly an operation might be, and what if it didn't help me see?"

"Has Jeremy made an appointment?"

"Yes, for this Friday."

"Take one day at a time," Ida advised.

\*\*\*\*

Dr. Apsley squeezed stinging eye drops into Abbey's eyes. She blinked several times and gripped the arms of the chair nervously.

"The drops will enlarge your pupils and allow me to see the back of your eye more clearly," he explained to both Abbey and Jeremy.

Her hands folded in her lap, Abbey was filled with a strange mixture of hope and anxiety. *Will I be able to see? Will the treatment be painful? Will I be able to look into Jeremy's eyes and watch him smile? Will I finally know what color is?*

After several minutes, the doctor examined Abbey's right eye with a bright light and then the left.

Though Abbey could see nothing, she could feel the heat of the light.

"You've been blind from birth?" Apsley asked.

"Yes," Abbey replied.

"I hoped perhaps that you suffered from congenital

cataracts because some surgeons are experimenting with cataract removal. But I'm sorry to say you appear to have damage to the optic nerves."

"What does that mean?" Jeremy asked.

"I'm afraid that at this time we have no cure for Abigail's condition."

Abbey swallowed back her disappointment. "Thank you," she said in a quivering voice.

"I'm very sorry. But I want you to know that new discoveries are being made every day, and progress will continue here and in Europe. What is not possible today could be possible in the future."

Abbey nodded, not trusting her voice to answer without faltering. Though she had tried not to get her hopes up, the disappointment was staggering. Once they'd left the physician's office, she remained uncharacteristically quiet. Outside on the street, life continued as usual. She heard carriages roll by, smelled horse sweat and leather, and heard the conversations of pedestrians.

"Are you turbly upset?" Jeremy asked.

She smiled as always at his pronunciation of "terribly." "I shouldn't have built up my hopes. You warned me not to," she said. "I wanted to see for you. I don't want to be a burden to you. I wanted to see our children one day and to know what color is."

Jeremy took her in his arms right there on the street and enveloped her in warmth. "This feeling right here, right now, is red," he said. "It's warm and vivid, full of life like the blood that gives us life. And ya could never be a burden. I love ya, Abbey. Don't ya know that?"

"Red," Abbey repeated. "So love is red."

Chapter Nineteen

Ida pulled back thick strands of Abbey's auburn hair, entwining them into a long French braid. Lucy stood on a chair to make herself tall enough to put white flowers into the braid.

"I don't want to be late to St. James's," Abbey said.

"We're not going to be late," Ida said. "I've got one eye on the clock and one on your hair. Now, let's get you to step into your wedding gown."

"Oh Ida, thank you for telling Aunt Agatha you'd help me get dressed. I'm glad she's meeting us at the church. She makes me a nervous wreck."

"I guess she means well," Ida said. "We'll arrange the veil at St. James's. Let me see if the hansom cab is outside." She crossed to the window. "It is!" She helped Lucy down from the chair swinging her around just to hear her giggle.

\*\*\*\*

Jeremy stood before the small mirror and scraped his face with the razor's sharp blade leaving behind smooth skin. *I don't want to scratch Abbey's tender skin when I kiss her.*

Shawn entered the room and slapped him on the back. "It's ya big day. Nervous?"

"Nah," Jeremy replied.

"She's a pretty colleen. Hope ya'll both be very

happy. Mam's spirits have certainly picked up."

"Ya stand by me and keep up with this ring." Jeremy took the gold band with the single pearl from his pocket and gave it to his brother. "It belonged ta Abbey's mother. Agatha gave it ta me last night. Brought it all the way from Arbor. It's sort of like her white flag of surrender."

"A peace offering of sorts?"

"Yes."

"Well, ya'd better hurry up if we're going ta catch the one o'clock ferry."

"Mam's dressed?"

"And ready ta go."

\*\*\*\*

In an ivy-covered alcove to the right of the sanctuary, Agatha fussed with Abbey's veil. "I wish your father were here to see you today." She blinked back tears, overcome by emotion.

"Yes," Abbey said. "I wish he were here to give me away, but I do feel his presence, I really do."

Agatha hugged her niece. "Her hair is lovely," she complimented Ida.

Ida cracked the door and peeked inside the church. "The sanctuary is full. Matron Bards has all the children and teachers here. I see the Rembolds. The organist is starting the prelude."

The organ music soared up through the pipes like an angelic choir.

"Jeremy and Shawn are coming up the aisle. What a handsome pair."

"Auntie, you'd better go now and slide into the pew."

Her aunt's lips brushed her cheek, and she

departed, running into her husband in the corridor.

"Is she ready?" Jack asked, bit stiff in a suit when he was so accustomed to farm clothes. He smiled anyway, proud to walk with his niece down the aisle.

"Yes," Abbey said and stepped into the hallway, taking her uncle's arm. She carried a single white rose. Ida and Lucy scurried ahead of them to seats on the back pew.

"You look lovely, child," he said, patting her hand. "Come with me."

Abbey walked with Jack to make her entrance into the church as Mendelsohn's *Wedding March* reverberated from the pipe organ.

*Oh Jeremy, I wish I could see your face.* She knew only that he was at the right side of the altar.

As though reading her mind, Uncle Jack bent closer and whispered in her ear, "The groom looks positively entranced. And you, my dear, are radiant."

Uncle Jack moved with her up to the altar and then transferred Abbey's arm from his own to Jeremy's.

"Dearly beloved, we are gathered here today to join this man and this woman in the Holy Sacrament of Marriage symbolic of the mystical union of Christ and his church. It is not to be entered into lightly but with reverence," Father William intoned. "In the name of the Father, the Son, and the Holy Ghost."

Abbey and Jeremy crossed themselves, and then Jeremy reached over and took her hand rubbing his thumb gently across her soft skin. Abbey tingled with happiness, pleasure, and reassurance.

When the mass concluded, Jeremy tenderly raised her veil and pulled her to him for a spectacular kiss that sent a shiver of anticipation down her spine. The organ struck up a dramatic chord, and the two of them moved together up the aisle, no longer two but one, in mystical union.

The guests followed them to the festive church hall where, thanks to the supervision of Carrie Rembold and Matron Bards, a delicious reception awaited. Jeremy described the two-tiered wedding cake, the chains of greenery and flowers that the Pearson students had made and hung, and the cut-glass punch bowl on the lace tablecloth.

Shawn offered his congratulations and kissed Abbey lightly on the cheek. "My new sister," he said.

"Everything went perfectly," Ida said, taking Abbey's hand.

"Oh Shawn, this is my best friend, Ida Allen," Abbey said as an introduction.

"It's a pleasure to meet you," Ida said with a smile.

"I assure ya, the pleasure is all mine," Shawn said, turning on the Irish charm.

"Be careful with this one," Jeremy warned Ida. "He's kissed the Blarney stone."

But Abbey heard sincere admiration for her friend in his comment.

"Would ya like ta sit with your aunt and uncle?" Jeremy asked. "They seem to be getting better acquainted with Mam."

She nodded.

He led Abbey to their table near the window where sunshine poured inside the room.

"She's a lovely girl," Abbey heard Mary McKetcheon saying to Aunt Agatha. "Lovely and gentle as springtime."

"Here they are now." Jack stood and pulled out a

chair for his niece.

Abbey sat and arranged her skirts around her. A single violinist began to play an Irish reel, and many of the guests made a circle to dance. Abbey clapped along in time with the music. Jeremy tapped the toe of his right foot. The blind children seemed to be enjoying themselves especially when slices of cake were passed around. Lucy appeared with a dab of vanilla icing on the tip of her perky, freckled nose.

Jeremy scraped it off with the tip of his finger. She giggled. *It'd be lovely to have a cute little girl like Lucy one day.*

"Shawn seems interested in your friend Ida," Jeremy confided to Abbey in a low tone. "They're talking together in a cozy corner."

"She'd be good to him," Abbey said. "She's been like a sister to me."

"Doin' a bit of match-making?"

"I just want everyone to be as happy as we are." She smiled. "What time are we going back on the ferry tonight?"

"We're not going back," Jeremy said. "I have a surprise for you. We're staying in Boston tonight at the Emerald Inn."

"Oh, that sounds turbly romantic." Abbey teased him by imitating his accent. "I'm afraid I can only afford one night. We'll go back ta the island tomorrow."

"To start the rest of our lives," Abbey said.

"Ta start the rest of our lives," Jeremy said, taking her hand and squeezing it. "Tagether and for always."

# Discussion Questions for Abbey's Tale

1. Why do you think Jeremy was attracted to the light-keeping job on a remote island?
2. Why is Abbey, who is blind, able to "see" more in Jeremy than sighted people can see?
3. How does Aunt Aggie misjudge Jeremy, and why is she concerned about Abbey marrying?
4. Why does Abbey believe that many men would not consider her a desirable wife?
5. Why does Everett who is blind and deaf have many behavioral problems? How does Bailey help him?
6. What skills does Abbey have that surprise Jeremy? Do people prejudge the blind?
7. How do Abbey's other senses help her survive in the forest when she's hiding?
8. What issues are brought up about Protestants and Catholics? How does Uncle Jack feel about the differences?
9. What prejudices toward Irish immigrants are evident in *Abbey's Tale*? What were conditions like on the coffin ships?
10. Why is it cathartic for Jeremy to join with other veterans to heal his inner scars?
11. Why did Jeremy fight for the United States? Was it patriotic or necessary for financial survival?
12. How does Gregory justify his illegal activities?
13. How does Gregory's defending lawyer try to exonerate him?
14. Why does Jeremy have mixed emotions about Abbey's possible healing from blindness?
15. Do you think his insecurities are warranted?
16. Which character seems to be attracted to Ida

Thompson near the end of the book?

17. Do you think Abbey is capable of being a competent mother or would her disability endanger her children?

18. Do you think being born blind would be more or less difficult than being born sighted and later losing one's sight?

## A word about the author...

Katherine McDermott has worked as an English teacher, guidance counselor, and adjunct English professor. She loves reading. She is married with two children and two adorable grandchildren. In her spare time, like her heroine Teresa in *Hiding*, she likes to paint with acrylics.

She received the Excellence in Christian Writing Award from the Blue Ridge Christian Writers Conference, the Daphne du Maurier award for an unpublished suspense novel, and honorable mention in the SOLA Romance Writers Conference.

She has written both fiction and non-fiction for magazines and newspapers. She is the author of two children's books, *The Underwear Tree* and *Les Petits Gardes*. She co-authored *The Lighthouses of S.C.*, wrote *All Work, All Play*, and has authored two plays.

~*~

Visit Kim McDermott at:
www.kmcdermottauthor.wordpress.com
www.katherinemcdermott.blogspot.com
amazon.com/author/mcdermottkatherine
www.amazon.com/author/kimmcdermott

# Other Books by This Author

If you enjoyed *Abbey's Tale*, you may also like *Hiding*, a suspense romance that won a Daphne du Maurier Award from RWA. It is also available from The Wild Rose Press, Inc.

## About *Hiding*:

Teresa Worthington escapes her abusive boyfriend, Alex, and flees to Paris to pursue a dream career in art. Alone and wary of men, she gradually makes friends and explores her new home. She is distraught to learn that Alex is still stalking her but is determined to create the life she has always wanted.

Handsome, compassionate, and brave, Serge Gervais, a young Frenchman, slowly wins her trust. He shows her the sights of France and promises to protect her from Alex. Teresa finds herself falling in love for the first time, until the unspeakable happens. Alex tracks her down and forces her into the catacombs beneath the city. Will Serge find Teresa in time to prevent Alex's vengeance?

www.ingramcontent.com/pod-product-compliance
Lightning Source LLC
Chambersburg PA
CBHW060934180626
46817CB00004B/1527